Also by Valerie Lillis

Table of Contents

Also by Valerie Lillis

The Nephilym Chronicles
Nephilym
Weight of the Crown
Cursed and Forgotten
Whispers of the Abyss
Sanctity of Blood
The Red Knight Adventures
The Red Knight
Homecoming
Haunted
Grimm Retellings
To Bloom in the Shadows
Requiem of a Queen
The Golden Fox

The Golden Fox

A Grimm Retelling

Valerie Lillis

Copyright © 2025
Valerie Lillis

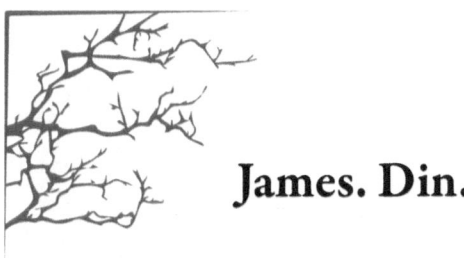

James. Din.

Thank you both for not only helping me find the will to rewrite this book, but for helping me through my darkest year to date.

The Golden Fox

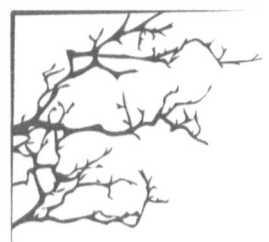

Chapter 1

Adrian Fultham raised his hands and reached within himself to the energy that flowed between all living things. In golden tendrils, it wrapped around him with a warmth rode the line between comfort and discomfort. With a flick of his wrists, he funneled the energy from himself to the tattered curtains that framed a window long since shattered by spring storms.

Controlling the magic was much like spinning thread; too little power and the thread snapped, too much and the thread became unstable with lumps of power. When he was careful, like he was now, then he could spin the magic into threads that could mend cloth, stone, or even flesh. The fabric came together slowly, the air wavering between him and the curtains with each pulse of energy. Threads of cotton formed, repairing and strengthening what had been frayed by time and nature. Holes were filled and tattered edges mended. Finally, faded colors were brightened as if the cloth had just been dyed weeks ago instead of decades.

Adrian's usual use of magic was keeping tabs on the goings on of his house, but he enjoyed the challenge of creation magic. Something like broken pottery required an entirely difference process. For a broken cup, the shards had to be reverted into clay so that all of the pieces could be rejoined together, then the cup had to be magically fired again to return it to a finished state. It was useful, especially when the treaty allowed for only the most minor repairs of the five noble houses. Even if they could sneak a few timbers for damaged walls, mending with magic was too exhausting for most spell-workers to handle.

Even with the additional magic afforded to him by his blood, Adrian felt the drain eat at him. He surveyed his work, noting the weave that he had created was looser than that of the original material. The next curtain he repaired, he would have to keep that in mind. Perhaps fixing one small hole first would let him correct the weave for the rest of the piece.

The window, like many of the others, could only hold the wind and rain at bay by wooden shutters. The glass, once a point of pride for the family, had long ago cracked and fallen through. There were a few shards trapped in the frame, shards so small that Adrian hadn't noticed them until he leaned against the window frame.

He pulled back sharply, looking from the pinpoints of blood under his arms to the window. Some of his blood had been left behind on a jagged piece, giving him an idea. Blood was a material just like any other, and the blood of spellworkers was potent as a source of magic. Raising his hands again toward the window, he focused on the shards.

Glass, it turned out, had a much different feel to magic. It was hard, but brittle. Solid, but not. It was as if a sea of crystals had been frozen in time, the flow and depth captured in a single moment. In that frozen sea was a memory: it was of a time before the piece was cracked and broken. Golden energy flowed from his shallow wounds, the cuts closing as the blood was burned away by the magic. Taking hold of the memory was like summoning a ghost; it had its own memories of other ghosts, with each new ghost having it's own collections of memories.

The shards responded to the memories and the energy mimicked the shards. Slowly, like new limbs on a tree, new glass began to form from the aether he only new as the Shom. What was once a ghost became real, and the colors of stained glass began to fill and return to fill the space.

"Adrian."

What glass he had managed to form crumbled away. With a sigh, he turned to the matron of House Fultham. His mother was neither tall nor short but held the remarkable trait shared by all Fulthams—eyes the color of molten gold. They were a color shared by him and his sister. Now those eyes were looking at him with thinly veiled trouble.

"Adrian, please," his mother continued. "Let the house keepers do their job and come with me."

"Is there something the matter?" There was always something the matter; taxes needed to be paid to a king, servants needed fed and paid, and Lily's visions needed to be interpreted. He hated that she took so long to get to the point of what she needed. Nonetheless, he kept a soothing voice—rushing her would only drag the interaction out making it take longer before he could fix the issue and return more personal pursuits.

"We need to get you ready. Matron Feyse has requested directly that you take the shoshyuh blessing for her house."

Adrian paused in the doorway of the sitting room. His mother flitted about, straightening books and ringing a bell for tea. "What?"

"Don't pretend deafness, I have enough on my plate with Lily. You have been chosen by the Matrons to become the shoshyuh for House Feyse. The ritual will be tonight and we have much to prepare."

"I refuse." He was the last heir. He couldn't just be sold to serve another house.

"By the Sisters," he mother said, turning sharply. "You can't refuse. It would shame our line."

Adrian crossed his arms, shaking his head as his mother sunk into a nearby chair. She rubbed her temples as if they were having a disagreement over what to serve for dinner instead of the possible end of their house.

"This is a wonderful opportunity, Adrian." Her voice was soft, as if pleading would earn his cooperation. "House Feyse is without a shoshyuh and they have no spellworkers strong enough to fill the role. This speaks volumes about the strength of our line: two children of the same generation given the calling."

There could never be a house without a shoshyuh—the Pact of the Sisters demanded it for the sake of peace. Still...If Adrian went by precedence then his human body would be stripped of him and in it's place would be a form suited to the Feyse motif, an animal that is a hunter by nature. The exchange was that the magic he already possessed would swell, a process that could destroy a weaker body. Traditionally, it was a child of the house blood, but in the cases of infertility or premature deaths, other citizens could be used.

The first born was always sent to the King, tribute for losing a war no one had living memory of. The second was to become the heir of the house. Any other children filled the pact or worked the grounds. They were always chosen as children, young minds were the most malleable to the change. Those between the ages of three and five were the most preferred for their ability to not only survive the ritual, but to forget what and who they were before it.

Though...in the case of his house, Lily was chosen less because of the number of children and more because she was a twin: twins naturally had a strong connection to the Shom, and a female child naturally fit the role of "the maiden", the Fultham motif.

"You're leaving our house without an heir," he cautioned.

"Lily will provide." She waved a hand dismissively, but it was trembling. Her cheeks were pale, and her eyes kept looking anywhere but him.

"...if her gift did not take her womb like it did her voice."

"The ritual does not steal your voice, Adrian. It just..."

"It just turns you into a conduit for the Shom." He finished for her. "Mother, what does the Feyse have over you? Shoshyuh don't just die. They can't."

His mother stood, a blush of color rose to her neck and face as she threw her hands up. Still, she did not look at him. "Well this one did! And I'm honestly not surprised. The wolf was made of a consort, not of the bloodline. Nothing has been right since the bear—" She stopped, and pulled in a deep breath before lowering her arms. Finally she looked at him and met his gaze. Behind the shine of unshed tears, her golden eyes had become a void. His mother wasn't there—not mentally.

"By the blood we share, Adrian Fultham," the Fultham matron intoned. "You will perform the duties of your house; you will become the Feyse shoshyuh."

The command, empowered by a thin, unwavering line of Shom, tightened around him like a noose. Arguments died on his lips, the choice wasn't his any longer...it never had been.

Again his mother sank into her chair, a tear rolling down her cheek even as she began to tell him what he was to do for the ritual. It wasn't a pretty process, he knew that. No spellwork that affected living flesh was "pretty". But even though he knew the process, he was made to stop and listen. She couldn't let him feign ignorance, couldn't let him slip out of the ritual even though it was forbidden by the Pact of the Sisters to make a shoshyuh from an unwilling person.

It took well over an hour before he was released to prepare himself. Rage boiled in his veins, but he hid it behind a tense bow and a sharp turn that gave him no time to reveal his thoughts to her. The light touch of his mother's hand found his arm. She said his name, but he couldn't look at her. Not now. Not without breaking the thin veil of calm he had pulled over himself. She let him go and it took every ounce of his control to close the door gently behind him.

He knew little of how the other houses treated their shoshyuh. Rumors circulated the towns and villages and ranged from complete isolation to blissful pampering. The only consistent thread was that a shoshyuh was owned by the house it served. It was an artifact, an item of immense power and pride, not a human bound to eternal service. Lily, the Fultham shoshyuh, was the only shoshyuh allowed to retain a human form; despite her outward appearance, she was kept locked away, her visions used as a tool for the house, her freedom limited to whichever land needed a spell of health or protection. Even now, as he walked past tapestries riddled with moth holes and cracks in the old wooden floors, he had more freedom than her.

Not for long, he thought. The ritual was in less that twelve hours. Then he wouldn't see Lily again. He hastened his step. Lily would be were she was always kept between escorted outings, but seconds now felt like needles beneath his feet.

Lily's room was a small study filled to the brim with books on history, agriculture, and spellwork. Her bed and bathing areas were neatly tucked away behind painted paper walls, her clothes kept elsewhere for servants to bring to her as the occasion required. Today, she lounged on her reading sofa with a heavy tome. Her face was puffy and red, her cheeks still partially wet. When he shut the door behind him, she turned and the silent knowledge of what was happening passed between them as if she had been at his side when his mother gave the horrid orders.

The book was forgotten on the lounger, as Lily flung herself into his arms. Together the twins sunk to the floor, his silent tears falling into her golden waves. She was shaking her head, rubbing her tears into his shoulder. Her hands gripped his tunic tighter, wanting to sign but unable to let him go to do so. The rage that had seemed so all-consuming crumbled. In it's place was a pit of fear.

"I don't have any choice," Adrian said in a croaked whisper. "I'm being sent away."

She shook her head more fervently. Goosebumps raised over their arms, the Shom had been disturbed by their distress.

"I don't want to go." His breath came out in a foggy puff.

Reflexively, he held his sister tighter against the cold. Lily relaxed and turned to look at him with one watery eye revealing the deep gold of her iris had been divided by a silver ring of light. A vision had come upon her. Adrian tensed, and pressed her forehead to his, willing her magic to show him what she saw. He couldn't remember when they learned she could share her visions with him. Though it was an invaluable skill for the house, it had infuriated their mother to no end. He was the only one able to see the visions first hand, and thus was key to interpreting them.

When this one over took him, the room faded to black. The chill deepened. He lost feeling in all but his face. When he did see again, it was the golden fur of an animal shoshyuh. Blood seeped from it, soaking the ground and turning the grass crimson. He tried to move, tried to pull away, but nothing changed. Instead, the shoshyuh rose to stand on blood soaked paws. It turned, a red void of viscera greeted him where a head should have been.

"Remember what you are," a voice whispered through that void. "Meat and blood. Fuel..."

Lily pulled back, releasing him from the vision. A shudder tore through him. Death, it seemed, was the only outcome Lily could see for him.

The creak of the attic door sounded behind them, a serving maid's gentle voice summoned him to the event hall. Again, Lily signed at him not to go, to send someone – anyone – else in his place. It must have been a startling sight to see his sister so out of sorts as the servant gasped. Adrian wasn't thrilled about having to calm the servant as well as his sister, but it bought him time.

The amount of time he needed, however, was far more than what he could scavenge. It was cut even shorter when he shared

Lily's distress with their mother. He was barred from seeing her until after the ritual. Lily's frantic objections only strengthened her resolve, her haunted gaze absent of any remorse for sending a second child of hers to die.

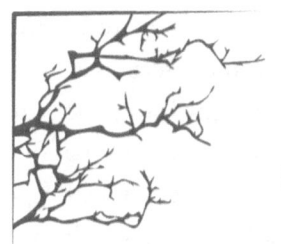

Chapter 2

Bound by his mother's will, Adrian walked into the room with nothing but a silver feather that Lily had braided into his short, chestnut hair. A farewell token—one that matched the feathers braided into his grandmother's hair on her burial day. It was the only thing they had convinced their mother to permit.

For all her bravado, the way she held herself with a stiff sense of purpose was enough to tell him someone was forcing her hand in this. Perhaps, if he cooperated, the answer would show itself. If he escaped and survived, perhaps he could even return home and remove whatever threat was being held over his family. It was a long shot with Lily's vision, but even if he was doomed to die, he could at least do something useful before the end came.

The ritual room was empty save for the salt mixed with dried herbs that had been poured around five lit candles. Four of the five candles were held by women of an ageless state, their golden amulets displaying their house symbol: the tree, the bird, the steed, and the beast. Behind him, his mother almost seemed a child compared to the other matrons for she lacked the lines of age on both her face and hair. Around her neck, the symbol of the maiden glittered in the candlelight.

Windows, small and barred, only gave enough room for the smoke to escape from the smoldering incense bowls. The four matrons that had been faceless to him until now did not seem like an avenue of escape either. His mother and two of the women seemed complacent with dull gazes that saw through him and everything else. One, elder Catherine of the Feyse, stared at him with what seemed to be a cruel satisfaction in her coal black eyes. The wolf-like beast on her amulet had been cast in a permanent snarl, but Adrian could swear it was watching him with pity.

The last, a thin woman bearing the symbol of the Oak, also held pity in her countenance; but it was a resigned pity. She could not, or would not, help him here. It sent a shiver down his spine when she gave him a consoling smile.

He stepped over the arcane writings on the floor. The mixture of fool's gold and magnesium spiraled and wound in the ancient language of the old kingdom and spoke of chains, terrors, and protections. At his mother's order, he stepped into the center of the writings and laid down. He suppressed a shiver, the chill of the stone bit through his clothes as surely as the heat of the arcane markings bled into him. it was old spellwork, slow to charge but dangerous in it's power. He should have known the markings would already be charged with magic. It was the only way to quicken the spell. Next would come the offering, one potent enough to strengthen the spell and bind it into the target.

Adrian knew what the offering was for a shoshyuh blessing. He had tried to prepare himself for it, but his stomach still twisted as the door opened to the whisper of bare feet on stone. He made himself look, made himself meet the fearful faces of the servants. There were two, a boy and girl that looked to have barely begun their entrance into adulthood. Together they kneeled on the edge of the circle, opposite of each other. Seeing him there, their heir, their lip strained to give him an encouraging smile. They would have chosen this, but that choice did not remove the fear from them. That fear, the haunted knowledge of what would come, stayed. It stayed as two blades appeared from the shadows to bite their exposed necks. It stayed as their heads were pulled back to allow blood and viscera to flow freely into the ritual circle.

And it stayed to haunt him as the ritual powder caught fire and blinded him. The world vanished in an array of white and black. Pain set deep in his bones as his body original body was burned away by the magic. His scream lost in the melodic chanting of the five matrons and the retched fumed of charred flesh. It was a small mercy that the world, with its horrors, faded away. But those faces, silent with the fear of death, haunted him even in oblivion.

As the transformation finished, the pain that throbbed through every sinew and bone returned. Adrian took one shuddering breath, and then another before coughing. A mass of gray and formless phlegm landed between his paws. The mass that had undoubtedly been part of his original body broke down further, becoming a gray pool of slime and then a smear of dust in the middle of the ritual circle.

He staggered to his feet, now covered in black fur that was rapidly changing to the gold typical of all shoshyuh. His claws scraped against the cracked stone. The room, already large, was now even larger. The five women towered over him, their candles nearly burned out as they chanted the final lines of the ancient incantations. The herbs that he had been able to smell on entering the circle, were now sickeningly pungent. Basil, rosemary, and sage blended with the burning of tallow and twine into a putrid attack on his senses.

The room tilted as Adrian's legs gave out beneath him. The ground was more forgiving to this smaller form. As expected, he had become a carnivorous beast of some kind, but his body was small, too small to be an adult wolf or bear. Adrian suspected the end result of his transformation wasn't as controlled as it should have been. The Shom had to remain flexible to merge with his soul.

With the ritual complete, they would be expected to bring the new shoshyuh to the feast where all of them could eat and regain their strength. Perhaps, if he was clever enough, he could find a way to slip away and find Lily. Whether or not she could do anything didn't matter as much as getting to see her one last time.

As one, the house matrons sagged. The matron of the oak gave a sidelong glace at the Feyse matron.

"That certainly took more energy than last time, Catherine," she said.

"You're just getting old." Catherine couldn't hide the fatigue that shadowed her just as much as the others. Unconcerned, the matron of the beast turned to his mother. "Marianne, my carriage is ready. It would be better to set out immediately."

The lack of emotion in her voice sent shivers down his back, causing his hackles to rise in a line from shoulders to tail. Adrian turned his head sharply, glaring at the beastly woman. Her agelessness had faded; wrinkles had deepened, her eyes had become far more sunken. The others, aside from his mother, also seem to have aged with the fatigue.

The woman with the branches in her hair exchanged a look with the two house matrons that had yet to comment. They shrugged and began cleaning up the ritual space.

"We've come this far to keep appearances," His mother said. "Let the shoshyuh enjoy the celebration before you take him home."

Adrian's ears flattened against his neck even as he tried to express gratitude to his mother. He wasn't sure what chance of escape he had attending the banquet, but it was a chance nonetheless. As he laid on the cold stone, Adrian couldn't help the sense of camaraderie he felt with old kitchen rags, those articles that scrubbed, rinsed, and were twisted until the edges had frayed to nothing.

The matron of the oak knelt beside him with a sigh. Her gentle scratches beneath his jaw, though unexpected, was not unwelcome. Andre hoped his clicking whine of appreciation translated well.

The elder gave him a sad smile. "If it's any consolation, Shushyuh Adrian, you make a very adorable fox."

A fox. So that was the form given to him. A warbling whine was all he could manage to show his gratitude. When he regained some strength, he needed to see if he could alter his form. If he could at least give himself the ability to communicate, his situation would improve.

The crone grit her teeth, a vein bulging along her jaw. A low growl, something he had never thought a human could do, did nothing to stop his attendant. "Stop coddling it, Ellen. That shoshyuh belongs to my house and I'll not have you turning it into a lapdog."

Ellen sighed and tucked a lock of silver hair beneath her branching hair ornaments. "A little less disdain would be a pleasant change, Catherine. We already know that the bear and the wolf didn't pass naturally, giving this little one, this young man, a proper send off is the least we could do before you take him."

Adrian's mother raised her hands, her face paling with more than fatigue. "Come now sisters. Let's retire this conversation. We are all tired. We should rest and join the feast before our frayed nerve-"

"Don't treat us like children, Mary." Ellen bent low, addressing Adrian in a soft voice. "Would you like to be carried out? I can only imagine the weakness you feel in your new body."

Adrian nodded and pressed his furred face into the palm of her hand. With little help on his part, he was picked up and carried out. With his muzzle draped on Ellen's shoulder, he had a very good view of Catherine's scowl. His mother gnawed at her lip, gaze bouncing between the two women with open unease. Perhaps, he thought, he wasn't as friendless as he feared. As it was, he felt Ellen's hand glide over his tail as they walked, tucking a slip of paper under the long shimmering fur.

The dining hall filled with people craning their necks to get a view of the shoshyuh. Servants came forward, assisting their small group in reaching their chairs. He was sat to the left of his mother, on a raised, cushioned stool. The crone took the seat to his left, keeping him in her periphery.

The jubilee died down. Up until now the guests had been treated with fine wines and crackers decorated with delicate cheeses and meats. Now the servants brought forth the main course of roasted ducks glazed in sunflower honey and mashed beets drizzled with a creamy dill sauce. As head of hosting house, his mother took the first bite.

At her nod the other house matrons raised their forks to follow and paused. Silence had fallen over the guests, their attention turned to the door. Lily had come, her lilac ribbons and pale gown a stark contrast against her olive-tan skin. Adrian didn't blame the guests for their response. This would be the first time in several years the Fultham shoshyuh had been seen by any visitor.

His mother's mouth twitched as she suppressed a frown, and Lily feigned any knowledge of their mother's displeasure. Her golden eyes were focused on him, never wavering as she came around the long table to stand behind his chair. As her hands reached down to partially cradle him, he leaned against her, hoping that without words she would feel his apology. He hadn't been able to escape, and he still had not found out if he even could.

She smiled sweetly down at him, tears barely restrained by her lashes. With a kiss on his nose, she left him to take the empty seat on the other side of their mother. The feast resumed, the chatter of the guests even more exuberant than before. He doubted anyone other than their mother recognized the gesture as a farewell.

What Adrian was sure his mother did not realize was what else was in that farewell. A spell, silent and small, had glittered like tears on her lashes just before the kiss goodbye. As they ate, the magic slowly took hold, establishing a strong hold. He let it, and by the time the next course of steamed vegetables and stuffed bread rolls were devoured, the blessing was in place.

'Can you hear me?' asked an unfamiliar voice in his mind. It was soft and lyrical in tone. Even though he had never heard his sister speak, he felt with a deep certainty that she was the voice in his mind.

'Yes,' He thought to her. Soft boiled eggs on a nest of shredded tubers were placed before him. After a cautious sniff, he started lapping up the yolk. 'How long will our connection last?'

'Not long, I would imagine. I've never given this blessing before.' She sipped on her water, pretending to focus on a gossip story across from her.

That made his tail puff out in anxiety. 'You haven't? What did you do?'

Blessings, the powerful spellwork that shoshyuh's were known for, were a science more than an art. Careful study and preparation had to be done before each spell, lest the magic go awry. Lily must have sensed his concern through the bond, as she continued:

'It's more of a wish. I wanted us to be able to talk, really talk, without others judging or stopping us. Then I combined that want with shom...I'm sorry I can't be more specific about it. I've been a shoshyuh for so long that spellwork for me is like moving any other part of my body.'

'Is there anything else you can tell me about these abilities? Maybe if I can master them quickly then I can escape.'

'I never need to use words or motions. When I desire something, I focus on how to achieve that goal while pulling the Shom into myself. Then I release it by touching the focus, or writing a name and casting the slip of paper into a fire.'

Adrian gnawed the white flesh of an egg while he considered the information. Shom was the essence of magic. It was the raw energy that magic was pulled from and spells were made from. Unrefined and untainted by human touch, it could be felt everywhere, and at the same instant existed nowhere. It was as if trapped behind an invisible curtain that separated their world from another.

Powers and abilities had come with his new status. With his sister having become a shoshyuh at the tender age of three years, there was much she knew, but couldn't fully explain. Their time together couldn't last forever, so she imparted what she could before the banquet ended.

The final bell rung too soon for either twin to be ready to part. The plates were taken away. Cups of water infused with sage and lemon were set before the guests to cleanse their palates. His drink was served in a bowl, the volume just low enough for him to avoid splashing the table. Lily sat back in her chair, eyes downcast as she sipped from her glass.

"We've dallied enough," the Feyse matron said, rising from the table. Her glare of suspicion bounced between the twins, as if she expected them to do something rash any moment.

Adrian's ears flattened against his head and neck. There was a glimmer of something other than suspicion—a hunger that made him curl his tail tight around his legs. He gave a low whine, causing nearby guests to look over and jokingly beg another few hours of the Matron's company. She wouldn't entertain even the nearest guest with a glance. Her gaze was for

Adrian alone, her tongue snaking out to wet her lips before she spoke again.

"Say farewell, little fox," she cooed and snapped her fingers to the waiting servants.

Two of them appeared, the symbol of the beast embroidered on their tunics. Between them was a crate lined with silk and containing a plush pillow. He suspected the interior was meant to save face rather than make his trip comfortable.

On the other side of his mother, tears dripped down Lily's cheeks. This was it. This was the end. But as he glanced again at his mother and sister, he couldn't accept the fate the box held for him. He jumped away from the box. Cups and candles went flying off the table as he jump again over his mother's cup and onto Lily's plate. The guests erupted in drunken laughter and delighted squeals. Lily could only give him a confused, sad smile.

With their eyes locked, he stood to place his front paws on his sister's shoulders. There was only one desire he had. He needed to know that she would be okay, that wherever he went he would know that she was alive and well. He knew she would want the same. His fur glittered and shone with a soft light, ruffling in a breeze that touched him and no other. The Shom, that mysterious energy he had always known, twisted into his will like fine wool spun into a thread.

A hush fell over the guests, their gaping mouths frozen. For a moment, time seemed frozen with them. The crone scowled, his mother clutched at her chest, and his sister stared at him in wonder, her tears not aligning with the half smile she wore. He touched his nose to hers, releasing the magic into her to carry out his wish. The strange breeze, the lights, and the timeless feel rushed away from him, rattling glasses and plates on the table.

Chaos erupted.

"Get him in the crate!" Feyse's shrill voice bounced off the walls, rattling windows and silencing the guests.

With a yip, he bounded away from his mother's outstretched hands. A nervous chuckle broke from the guests. Their attentions shuffled nervously between the fox to the matrons. Adrian leaned into their confusion, landing on the back of a chair to stick his tongue out at his mother. The longer the guests were confused, the less inclined they would be to interfere in his escape.

Chairs crashed against the wooden floors. The other matrons were standing to join the chase. Magic gathered in the air—thick, heavy, and charged. Adrian leapt away, splashing a glass of water over himself and the table. Flames ignited overhead while spreading over the floor below. Writhing chains slid over his fur as they missed him. A guard lept for him, gauntlets freezing just shy of his tail as vines mistook the blundering man as their target.

"Catch him already," Feyse screeched over the clamor of armor on stone.

His mother's eyes flashed with amber light. Scrambling onto the top of a candle pillar, Adrian let the flames lick his fur as he braced against the flow of magic. A serving girl stood in the shadows below him. With a flick of her wrist she opened the shutters wide. Stone garden paths glimmered in the starlight beyond this hellish room. Uneasy laughter turned to screams, the fire was uncontrolled. Rising, they clamored away toward the door. There was an opening, but with all the attention on him, it seemed impossible to take.

In his mind, Lily screamed for him to run.

He leapt. Above, the chandelier flickered. The stand behind him tilted. Candles fell out of their holders. And then the light, the fire, all was gone. Mere seconds later, The light of his fur tore away the darkness. One became nine, and behind it all, he dropped to the ground unseen. His fur was dark and translucent, his form little more than that of a shade.

One of the mirrors never made it to the chandelier; it died screaming—crushed by the chains. The other eight scrambled to escape scattering candles, napkins, and silverware all around the room. The vine caught the candles, the hot wax scorching the tender flesh. Flames, uncontrolled, were beginning to spread. Guests screamed, desperate to get away before they too were burnt alive. Guards, spells, and grasping hands all jumped to gather the foxes. Adrian, meanwhile, followed the faceless woman through the window and into the courtyard beyond.

Freedom, much like the sun, was still a long way off.

Adrian thought the most difficult part would be escaping the banquet, but as he lept into the garden he saw the house guards rushing toward the smoking building. The serving girl jumped through the window after him, lifting her skirts enough to hide him as she landed.

She moved at a brisk pace toward the guards, shouting that a fire had been started in the banquet hall. Once the guards were fully focused on the house, she allowed him to stand beneath the skirt to make it less obvious he was there. Beneath the fabric, he waddled around on his hind legs with a paw on the back of her leg for balance.

Adrian struggled to keep up with her. His furry little legs burned by the time she had reached the outer garden. To his relief, the garden was still empty, the attention still on the house. The serving woman didn't stop. With fear in each step, she hurried him away from the only place he had ever known into the forest beyond.

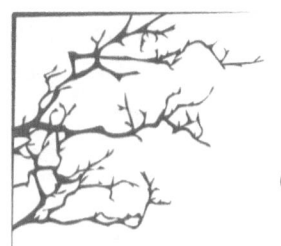

Chapter 3

Adrian coughed. The magic scalded his mouth and throat. The strain of morphing his anatomy to be capable of speech was unable to be soothed. They had made it. Through the courtyards and the side roads into the forest. He hadn't expected the woman to stay with him, he wasn't even sure which house she hailed from. But there she was, waiting patiently nearby as he crouched beside a brook for a drink.

The moon was high and full, illuminating a thin figure that was similar in age to him. Her hands twisted and trembled together as she waited. Words seemed to be bouncing just on the tip of her tongue behind lip pressed tightly closed.

"Apologies," he said as he moved to curl up on twigs and fallen leaves. How was the proper way to sit when one was a magic fox? He supposed there wasn't a handbook or lessons for him. He settled for crossing his front paws, his tail wrapped against his side in a relaxed manner. "I would have spoken earlier, but this form has its limitations."

Her eyes widened. Beneath her, forest detritus crunched and shifted as she sat against one of the ancient trees. Then she collected herself. "Yes...Of course. I...didn't expect you to talk. I've never known any shoshyuh to talk."

"I can only do so much with this body it seems. Was my predecessor, the wolf, also unable to speak?"

"Yes." She looked away briefly, a shadow of grief passing in the moment. "I became adept at understanding him without words."

So she was of House Feyse. Adrian attempted to maintain what he felt was a polite, nuetral posture, but he couldn't help the way his hackles rose. Perhaps this was some ploy to gain his cooperation, or to make his death even more plausible to the other four houses. "While I am eternally grateful that you helped me," he said slowly, "I'm curious to know why. It is very rare that a servant would act directly against the best interested of their house."

She looked down, watching her hands as she continued to wring them against her skirts. Adrian allowed the weight of the silence between them to press his rescuer. It didn't take very long for her to give. "I...didn't like seeing the shoshyuh of house Faltham cry..."

"My sister's tears drove you to betray your house?" It sounded ludicrous to him. Yet in the moonlight he could make out a blush of color across the woman's face and a embarrassed twist to her lips even though she wouldn't look directly at him. Just who was this woman, he wondered. There had to have been more to the story, something she was hiding under this affection she showed for Lily.

The silence stretched between them again, filled by the hum of nightlife. The woman sighed, her shoulders relaxing as she finally looked at him. He wasn't sure he had ever seen eyes that shade of green, so dark as to nearly be black except for the very edge which was so pale as to nearly be silver.

"I am Sarah, keeper of the Feyse shoshyuh. Don't go," she reached toward him as he made to flee. "I won't give you to her. Please, let me explain:"

"You were to be given a room in the Feyse courtyard; a small house to sheild you from nature, and a garden of your own to entertain you. Servants would bring you meals daily, I would tend to you ensuring you did not fall into too deep a melancholy and that your garden stayed clean. In exchange, you were to maintain a blessing on the Feyse lands for five years in order to ensure game was plenty for our hunters and trappers."

"Only five years? That seems a very short time."

"Yes, because that is how long it takes for the shoshyuh blessing to mature. Your form is still maleable right now. The Shom is unstable and your path uncertain. Each day that ticks by, the Shom and your soul align a little more and fit a little closer together. The spells you can cast will narrow down to a few powerful blessings, and the Shom will become intertwined with every part of you from your bones to your pelt. You would be a mature shoshyuh, one ready to be harvested for your magical potential."

She was watching him expectantly, as if her explanation had ended in a question. When he said nothing and continued to sit with his ears flat against his head and neck, she continued.

"My matron found that even if the shoshyuh dies, as long as it has matured, the blessing with stay concentrated in the body for several years. The flesh, if consumed, can even be used to enhance the shomnihi of people."

He blinked. His sister's vision came back to him: the darkness, the sharp smell of blood. Messing with the shomnihi, the connection between soul and magic, was dangerous. Several casters throughout history had sought ways to grow and strengthen that connection. Each one was driven mad. Powerful spellcasters had come from those times, but so too had the extinction of familiars. "Are you planning to harvest me yourself?"

Sarah's gave him a pained look, the tinge of illness crept over her. "I couldn't bear the task. I am simply trying to absolve the sins of my blood as Matron Ellen suggested."

Ellen. By the light of his fur, he teased the little note from his fur. It was about the width of his paw, the scrawling lines of text difficult to read in the dim light. Pulling a little more light into himself he read the tight lines of text.

Shoshyuh of the Feyse House, my congratulations and condolences. The Great Oak has told me a cruel fate. awaits you. You must escape or die. The Lake of the Thousand Souls and a friend will guide you.

He looked from the note to Sarah and back again. It made sense why Ellen would send a servant like Sarah. He wouldn't have trusted a noble in the chaos of the dinner. Seeking the Lake of the Thousand Souls, however, was not a simple task. He had heard of it but could never figure out where it was. It was an ancient power that survived the fall of the clans. Legend said that only the fruit of a shoshyuh given to the heart of the kingdom could awaken the slumbering spirit of the lake.

Sarah turned, looking deep into the forest shadows. Adrian couldn't see anything strange but Satah rose and motioned for him to do the same. "We can talk more later," she whispered. "Move. We need to keep going."

No riders pursued them as they ran through the moonlit forest. None appeared at dawn when they stopped to rest. Still, Sarah pushed for them to travel deeper into the woods, parallel to the road. With sleep as elusive as ever, they rested a little more than an hour before continuing on their way. Exhaustion caught them, with the thunder of hooves on the road.

"Quick, up that tree," Adrian hissed.

She did not hesitate. Branches snagged her dress, tearing it as she climbed up to the more densely packed branches. Adrian hoped the few scraps would escape attention and bolted into a shallow burrow.

The clatter of hooves grew to a thunderous roar; tremors traveled through the ground, the baying of hounds echoed with the screams of the dying. The riders came into view, human trappers clung to steeds armored in bone. Hounds of shadow led them.

The thunder of the horses faded as they passed. He waited. Nothing. They didn't turn. No secondary party followed behind

Adrian shuddered and slowly crept from his hiding place. A shoshyuh was too valuable a tool to be allowed escape. Perhaps she didn't care because she knew they wouldn't be able to get far. Adrian shuddered again, his hackles rising as he watched the hounds melt through shadows only to appear farther up the road.

It was only once the hunting party had travelled beyond his hearing that Adrian called Sarah from the tree. She was pale, trembling as she fussed at the jagged tears of her skirt. There was no hope of making those rips lay flat.

"Come on," Adrian said as he trotted deeper into the woods. "We can't stay here."

"We have no map and no way to know where the shadow hounds will go."

"Shadow hounds? You've seen those creatures before?"

Sarah nodded, wrapping her arms around herself as she stared at the empty trail the riders had left behind. "The last shoshyuh...he refused to lay down before her blade. She used them...hunted and killed him before he could fight back."

There was something else that hung in the air between them. It was a horror left unspoken but not unseen. She could never unsee it. And as he searched her face for answers, Adrian decided it was a secret he didn't want to know.

Turning from the road, Adrian dove deeper into the forest. Sarah's quick steps were soft as she kept pace. Barely a twig or leave was disturbed by their flight. Unfortunately, twisting brambles grew in dense patches through the forest floor. While the thorns did little to stop the fox from slipping through, they forced Sarah to discard her dress. Left with only a cotton slip and leather boots, she continued after him.

A clear stream wound through the trees, offering temporary respite. Smooth pebbles and rocks were visible even as they broke the surface and sent riffles babbling farther downstream. They both drank heartily from it.

"It's shallow enough to cross here," Adrian said, with water dripping from his muzzle. "Once across, we can follow it Northeast to the edge of the forest."

The land controlled by the five houses had a single true river. It cut through the middle of the territory, awkwardly dividing it between the houses. All streams, creeks, and springs fed the Great River and, as a result, the Great Oak where any knowledge could be gained.

"We are going to need to rest soon," Sarah said. "And I'm not fond of the idea of trekking through the woods in wet clothes."

Adrian raised a furry eyebrow. "You don't know how to magically dry your clothes? It's a common enough spell."

"I don't have magic." Red crept up her neck and across her cheeks. "Not everyone is as magically adept as the Fulthams."

He laid his ears back, leaning away from her. "Why are you upset? You're a house servant, all house servants have some ability to cast."

"Well I don't." She turned from him, crossing the stream without further discussion.

Ears back and tail low, he followed behind. The undergrowth was thickest near the bank of the creek. Brambles, thick grasses, and well hidden vines and roots picked away at what little energy they had left. Soon the cloud of fatigue had become too thick for crisp water to splash away.

Adrian didn't remember when their feet carried them from the forest floor onto a worn dirt road. Over the rut of wagon wheels and onto a dirt path they staggered. The tree line had become so thin they could see the farmland and sheep herds beyond the forest. Across the stream, a cottage stood just a stone's throw away.

Most homesteads were built using a combination of sticks and maud with woven thatch serving as a roof. This cottage was made of stone. Handsome logs framed the house and held up a roof of wooden shingles. Flowers and herbs overflowed from stone garden beds in an array of greens, purples, and yellows. With barely a glance his way, Sarah crossed the garden and rapped softly on the wooden door.

Adrian scrambled, hiding behind an old half barrel that had been filled with mums. A few of the orange blossoms fell, sitting on his head as an elderly woman opened the door.

"Oh," the elder said in surprise. "What happened dear? Oh, nevermind that. Come in, come in."

Sarah was pulled inside. The door swung to closed but didn't latch. Creeping forward, Adrian peeked inside of the modest little home.

The room was clean, the floor covered in furs and woven rugs over wooden planks. A tin kettle simmered over a small heart fire. There was a bed in the corner, and a door that led to somewhere else in the house. The elder sat Sarah beside the fire, helping her out of her soiled shift while chattering away about the weather and the garden. When Sarah was slow to engage in the idle chatter, a more pointed question was raised:

"Now, don't get upset at me for sticking my nose in your business, but...Why are you wandering so deep in the forest? And in your under clothes no less?"

Sarah hesitated, glancing at the open door. "Well, uh, I got separated from my group. I got turned around and lost in the forest."

"Oh? Where was your group heading? I may be able to give you directions."

"Oakton..."

"Oh! Well you're in luck then. Take a rest here and it'll be just a day's walk, maybe two to the North and you'll be there. Though, I am curious why a Feyse girl like yourself would be interested in visiting our city."

Color drained from Sarah's face. The elder didn't notice or didn't comment and fussed over her tangled hair. "We wanted to see the Great Tree," she said slowly.

"Ah, a pilgrimage," The woman nodded. "About time those happened. Back in my day, pilgrimages between the houses happened all the time. It was considered respectful for each Matron to visit all five of the shoshyuh every year. Well, back before the houses got to be so darn mistrustful of each other." With a sigh, the elder turned to grab a wooden hair comb from the mantle.

"All five?"

The elder nodded and continued with her stories of the olden days. There was much to hear about, and Adrian suspected they hadn't heard even half of the woman's knowledge before Sarah was cleaned, clothed in a simple dress, and fast asleep in the single bed. Adrian dashed back into hiding as the woman left Sarah to tend to the garden.

Her bones creaked and crackled as she bent over the plants, her fingers removing stray seedlings.

"I see a little fox in the mums," she said with a soft smile. He jumped and darted farther away. "Oh, don't run." she chided.

Adrian crept closer again, his ears flat against his neck and his body low to the ground.

"Ah," she said, still focused on her plants. "That's a good little fox. Do you think you could help an old woman with something? I have a stubborn root in the bed. The roses it blooms are beautiful, but it's choking out my lavender. Could you get my snips off the stool for me?"

Adrian blinked slowly, unsure if he had been found out, or if the old woman normally made requests of animals. He raised himself up to peer at the root she had partially dug from between two plants. It was thick, unable to be broken easily by hand. Against the wall, a small stool stood beside an empty wash basket; a pair of worn snips on the seat.

"Thank you little fox," she said, as he dropped the tool beside her free hand. "I knew a little critter like you once. It was a honey badger with golden stripes down his back. He followed my little Naevine everywhere. Helped her collect eggs and dig out the veggy patches...I always wondered what had happened to him after she passed on. He probably went to the old willow where they use to sleep the afternoon sun away."

One snip and she was able to dig out a root that was about a foot long that stretched from one bush to another. She placed the root aside and began to clean her shears. "I'll have to burn that later or it might regrow with a vengeance. Better it than the whole bush though. You should run and play, little fox. Your friend will be fine in my care. You might even go curl up with her, but only if you want. I know you critters have many good reasons behind your decisions."

With a parting smile, the elder stood and placed the snips back on the stool before disappearing inside with the root. Adrian stared after her, growing more and more uncertain about the sanity of the woman. Fatigue reminded him that he didn't have the energy for problem solving. With one last look at the cottage, he dashed off into the woods to rest out of sight in the nook of an elm's roots.

Rain pattered on the leaves, when he awoke. Hidden behind the dark gray clouds, the sun offered only dim lighting. Still half asleep, Adrian listened to the harsh whispers of the stream. His stomach growled, urging him up and out of the shallow burrow. There were plenty of puddles around his sleeping spot, but he padded past. The stream he trusted more, he also hoped to find small fishes on the bank, or some other animal he could stomach eating.

Unfortunately, there was no fish that he could see as he drank from the stream. There were a few insects, which were enough to stave off the hunger. The crunch of the shells and hardened bodies would have been satisfying, had the insides not been a slimy sort of soft. Again he drank from the stream, desperate to wash the taste from his mouth.

Compared to the deeper green of the elms that framed the stream, the blue-green leaves of a willow branch stood out as it floated by. Upstream, more of the hanging branches were peeking out over the water.

It was a honey badger with golden stripes...I always wondered what had happened to him...probably went to the old willow where they used to sleep...

Adrian trotted along the bank, cursing his earlier fatigue. Had he been more alert, he would have been able to pay attention. True gold fur was rare—now only found on the shoshyuh animals. Familiars, those with a naturally high shomnihi could have gold or silver markings. Animals with those markings appeared in many legends with abilities ranging from speech to controlling plant growth and affecting the weather.

The badger could very well have been one such creature. Beneath the tree, his suspicion grew. Welts raced along the trunk and boughs of the willow, years of healing unable to completely erase the prayers and spells that had been carved into its flesh. At the base of the tree,cradled by sprawling roots, was the entrance of an old badger sett.

Adrian crept up to the opening, peering down into the darkness. More scratched prayers lined the hard packed opening, faded to an unrecognizable scrawl with age. There were no scents aside from that of damp soil and insects. Not even the smell of decay was present to warn him of the skeleton that lay in the first chamber. It lay curled up in what remained of a mixture of black and gold tufts of fur. The skull, intact except for a single tooth in the front, stared at him with wide, empty sockets.

His fur stood on end as he crept around the edge of the room. The skeleton was larger than him, but unmoving. Behind it was another tunnel that was longer than the first. The dim lighting of the rainy afternoon was left behind in that first room, leaving Adrian to his limited night vision as he descended into the sett.

Artifacts of various shapes and sizes littered the floor of the second room. Scraps of cloth, and a small, dingy blanket formed a nest in the center. Pebbles, tool handles, and small wooden carvings were scattered around. In the middle of it all was a small thin box, or book, wrapped tightly in faded yellow cloth. At the back of the room was another opening, this one short enough for the strips of leather inside to be visible.

Curious, he began to paw and nose through the room. The carvings were crude, barely recognizable as basic animal forms.

One of the better ones looked similar to a badger, and had a yellow ribbon tied in a bow around its neck. The nest was dusty, but otherwise clean, with its package wrapped tightly. The leather belonged to a harness. Bags and baubles were tied to it, and it seemed to be of a construction that allowed an animal like Adrian or the Badger to don or doff the harness at their leisure.

Old stories told of familiars that bonded to humans, becoming their shadow and most loyal companion. Surrounded by the mementos of such a relationship, Adrian pitied the creature. The dead, however, had no use for his pity.

Once laid out on the floor, the harness looked like it could be adjusted to his size. He tried it, sliping each loop and pad over his body before using his teeth to tighten the straps. It was a tedious process. But once he had tightened the harness down, the straps did not move.

The only other items he took from the room were the package, which he suspected was a journal, and the wooden badger, which he left beside the skull of the former resident. Hopefully, the small gesture would keep the badger's soul from haunting him. Securing the journal in a side pouch of his harness, Adrian returned to the cottage.

Cracked ruins and an overgrown garden where all that stood in the place he had left the cheery little cottage.

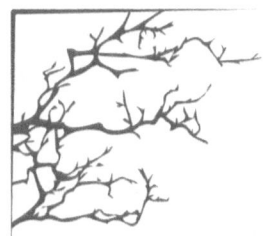

Chapter 4

His pounded against his ribs as he darted into the structure. The door was lying shattered inside, the roof was full of holes where sections of rotted wood had fallen through. A rusted pot hung over a cold hearth dusted with ash.

On the remains of the bed, Sarah slept soundly clothed in a simple green gown over a clean and dry shift. At his concerned yip, she started awake, then screamed as she scrambled off the bed. The slumbering skull of a human shifted, knocked loose by her frantic movement. The rest of the body remained undisturbed beneath the worn cover.

Sarah's legs shook as she rose to her feet and looked around the dusty and web filled room. "What is this? What did you do?" She looked at him, her eyes wide from shock.

Adrian shook his head. "I didn't do anything. At least, I don't think I did."

"Let's get out of here then." Sarah pulled on her shoes before moving to leave the house.

"Wait," he hopped in front of her, blocking the path to the door. "We need to figure out our next moves."

"We can figure out details when we get to Oakton. The tree knows everything."

He shook his head. "I don't think we should risk approaching the tree yet. If Matron Ellen is suspected at all in helping us, we'd only be dooming her."

"So...what?" She crossed her arms, shuddering as she glanced around. "We just wait in a cursed house in the middle of the forest until you decide where to go next?"

He snorted in irritation. Sarah could try thinking of ideas of her own. "Yes, we'll wait here. At least until morning. There's probably some firewood around here somewhere, get a small pile together. I'll look around the rest of the house."

She huffed an exasperated sigh, but moved to do as he asked. At least it would keep her distracted.

Putting his nose to the ground, Adrian began exploring the building. Even though the roof had long since fallen in, the stone walls stood strong. The scent of mice and other forest rodents was more than a few days old. The smell of the elderly woman, to his surprise, was gone, as if she had never been there. That concerned him. It concerned him even more that the few gray locks of hair that clung to the resting skull.

The door beside the bed had no lock. At a gentle nudge, it swung open as if welcoming him inside. The squeal of the rusted hinge earned him an irate look from Sara as she brought him an armful of soggy logs. Rain had come, and it had no intention of stopping. At her request, he used magic to start a small hearth fire before slipping into the side room.

The room beyond was coated in a layer of dust twice as thick as the rest of the house. A window, the shutters long rotted away, let in the trickling rain which pooled at the foot of a rocking chair. At its side was a long woven basket suspended between sturdy crossed planks. Without wind or touch, the basket swayed and from it the soft wail of a baby began.

Adrian backed away, his hackles rising from neck to tail. The chair beside the basket moved, rocking back and forth with a slow cadence. A woman, little more than a fuzzy outline leaned forward in the chair and gathered the invisible child in her arms. Together they rocked. A golden mist shimmered at the foot of the chair; an indistinct mass of a large animal curled at their feet. Adrian jumped when the woman spoke:

"Hush, my little love. It is alright. Oo, I know the rain is spooky. But the rain is a good thing."

The child shuffled, its disgruntled grunts and short whines quieter now.

"Yes," the woman continued. "I'm absolutely certain. It will bring flowers and help leaves grow on the trees, and when you're older I'm sure you'll love to play in the mud. It will be great, my little love. You'll see."

The images and sounds faded away. The infant vanished first. Then the woman faded away. The creature looked up, meeting Adrian's gaze with golden eyes. A golden stripe shimmered from the phantom's head to it's tail. With a silent nod of acknowledgement, it also faded back beyond the veil of the Shom. When nothing else appeared, Adiran cautiously crept forward. There were no smells to indicate anyone had been in the room, not even that of forst animals. The dust, thick on both basket and chair, was left undisturbed.

He crouched where the creature had been, shivering at the chill the phantom left behind. With one leap he was in the rocking chair, scrambling for purchase in the dust. Once it's rocking slowed to a stop, he reached up to peer into the swinging basket. Dust covered blankets partially filled the basket, an imprint of a small body in the center of the arrangement. He was about to climb back down when light glinted off something partially hidden by the fabric.

A pewter locket strung from a strip of cloth. The front held the design of a sprawling tree whose branches reach so far down as to tangle with its roots. On the back was an inscription too caked with dirt to read in the dim light. As he slipped the item into his bags, something small rattled and clinked inside.

On the other side of the small room were the remains of a bed. To Adiran's relief, there was not a body. There was, however, a small knife and shapeless chunk of wood beside the bed. With nothing else to see, he slipped away and firmly shut the door behind himself.

"Anything interesting?"

He jumped, spinning around to see Sarah by the fire. The log she had been holding clattered to the floor as she jerked back at his sudden movement. Adrian shook his fur out, trying in vain to dispell the chill from the nursery. It wouldn't help either of them if Sarah knew there had been actual ghosts in the other room.

"Sorry," he said as he curled up beside the fire.

"Okay...What did you find?"

"Another bedroom. It hadn't been used in a long time."

"uh-huh..." she said, the tone indicating she wasn't sure she wanted to know what else he found in there. Casting a cautious glance at the door to the back room, she settled beside him to tend to the fire. "And the fox-sized harness?"

"Badger-sized, actually. The..." He glanced back at the skeleton. Its empty sockets were glued to them. "...lady talked to herself in the garden. Apparently her daughter was friends with a familiar."

Sarah's eyebrows raised in disbelief. He didn't blame her, familiars had been gone for so long they were thought to be local legends by most people. What rested in the sett, however, didn't leave room for doubt. Cautiously, he extracted the package from his bags and scratched at the cloth until the worn leather it protected was revealed.

The journal was palm wide, and a hand in length. Spotted beveling decorated the cover with the shape of a badger. Excitement bubbled up, sending his tail to thud repeatedly against the floor. He stretched out, prepared for a lengthy session of reading. Flipping the cover open, that excitement fell into dismay.

Sarah started at his sudden bark of frustration. "What?"

"It's written in Hisali."

"And that's a problem? I thought you were the heir of your house."

Adrian shook his head in irritation, staring at the scrawling lines of text. Hisali was an old tongue, now only spoken by the direct descendants of the five houses if at all. He and his sister had both learned it, as it had become integral to their connection to the Shom and thus their ability to cast magic.

It was the language of the old courts, of advisors, kings, and queens. The scrawling text before him was not the same. It was in shorthand, with partial words and phrases mixed with punctuation in odd ways. It reminded him of the way servants spoke when they didn't think anyone else was around.

Sarah leaned over him and wrinkled her nose at the sloppy writing. "Ugh, how is that Hisali? You'd get better use burning it for heat than trying to read it."

He bared his teeth, growling as she reached for the book. Despite his small size, the display was enough for her to jerk away. Licking his lip, he returned to staring at the pages. "A wise man might rest on a headstone between travels. A foolish man curses the grave and runs away," he said softly. "I will decipher this, if only to know who the familiar and girl were. And then I will continue to keep it safe."

That night, Adrian read by the light of the fire—or tried to. In addition to the unfamiliar dialect, the handwriting was cramped and small. Every available inch of paper was covered. Sketches of badgers, flowers, and trees broke through like islands of respite for tired eyes. A few of the words he understood, which he used to start piecing together phrases, and then sentences within the diary. And it was a diary, told from the perspective of a young woman who went on woodland adventures with her familiar.

It almost seemed too mundane. But the more he held the book beneath his paws, the more he knew it was anything but. His fur glowed as he pulled the Shom into himself. Punctuation vanished, words untangled themselves, and the images moved subtly as if the sketches were living beings. The spells of the young woman came to the forefront. The day to day toil of her life melted into the background.

The pages almost seemed to shimmer as Adrian channeled his energy into the journal. Words once hidden, came to life in a glittering sliver ink on the page.

As above, where birds fly free.

As below, where foxes sleep
Hear me friends today and tomorrow,
Where the Shom is unknown, so I must go.

It was a spell and a song, woven together by ancient magic. The strands were crude, but powerful, the intend pure. The text over the top spoke how the badger taught the girl. It was, according to the badger, incase she was ever alone and in need of friends great and small. Adrian hummed a tune he had heard his grandmother sing in the past. When he found a way to fit the words together, he sang it softly to himself.

The Shom responded lazily at first, starting as a flicker of warm that grew into the merry heat of a hearth fire. The soft glow of magic raced through his fur making it stand on end. He sang it again. The glow became trails of light that raced around him. The third time he sang the words, the lights raced away. The dark cloaked him once more.

The silence ticked by. It pressed against him as he strained to hear something—anything that told him if the spell did as it said. Through the windowsill, the shadows pressed close...then receded from the ruined cottage.

Hooves clipped softly on the forest floor. A mane of silver hung over the slender ebony form. Youth gave life to her steps while golden fur painted her forelegs in socks. It was a horse, too young to have foaled, too old to be called a filly. A glimmering golden feather hung where it had been braided into the horse's hair. Adrian's jaw slackened. The spell had worked.

"You have a nice voice," the horse said as she approached. "My name is Ivy. What's yours?"

"Adrian. Do you know that song?"

Ivy snorted, blowing out a short laugh. "Not at all. It felt right to follow, so I did. Papa says it's important to follow what feels right."

Behind Ivy, down was breaking over the forest. He had spent all night with the journal. Sarah, who had spent the night tossing and turning on the floor, sat up when she heard the voices. Rubbing her eyes, she looked from Adrian to the horse and dropped her hand in her lap. The way she seemed too stunned for words drew a bubbly knicker from their guest.

"Ivy here is a familiar," the fox explained. "She's a friend."

"Yay, friends," the mare whinnied. "I've never had a human or a fox as a friend. What are we going to do first?"

"I think...we are going to go on a journey."

"Like an adventure? So exciting. What should I call you though? Papa said friends should always know each other's names."

"Oh? My name is Adrian," he said before motioning with his head to his companion. "And, this is Sarah."

"Adrian and Sarah." The mare pranced from foot to foot, her silver mane and tail bouncing with the movements. "Okay, where are we going? I love adventures."

"The barrows."

Sarah gave him a incredulous stare. Where the Thula had their aviaries, and the Huve their farms and horses, House Fultham had the barrows. Tall hills that formed a tiny mountain chain along the eastern most border. It's where his grandmother had been buried as well as every Fultham matron before her.

With Sarah's fear of ghosts, he understood her anxiety about the location. But he had his reasons. There were ghosts in this kingdom, ghosts that might be able to get him some answers. If ghosts could share ancient magic with him through the Shom, perhaps they could share other things—like the spell for reversing his blessing.

Ivy lowered herself to her knees, allowing Adrian and Sarah to climb on her back. There was a thick blanket strapped to her in place of a saddle, though no harness or bit to guide her dash from the stable. Adrian dug his claws into the fabric, praying it to be enough to hold. Stars darkened to black spots in his vision, threatening a loss of consciousness from the jostling. Faintly, he heard the songbird's cry directing them East, to the burrows.

Ivy apparently knew of the barrows as well, as the little filly began to skip and prance through the forest, each step punctuating the line of a nursery rhyme:

The barrows, the barrows
To the east are the barrows
Tall ones, short ones, all in a row
There the dead sleep.
There the dead dream.
And little spirits sing so sweet.

Sarah shuddered, hugging herself as if to dispel some chill. "I'm, not particularly fond of graves. Is there somewhere else we could get information? Perhaps an old journal hidden under a floorboard or something..."

"The barrows aren't graves," Ivy giggled. "They're beds for the dead to dream! Papa said so. He said the golden wraiths sing them to sleep while they wait for those in need."

"Your father said that?" Adrian tilted his head. Perhaps the souls of past Fultham Shoshyuh could also be found there.

"Papa would never lie. He says lying is beneath us."

Sarah looked away from the two of them. "My father said lies keep us alive."

Ivy snorted. "Well that was silly."

"Every family has their dark secrets," Adrian cut in as he felt Sarah tense behind him. He didn't need a fight between the only two people that had been able to help him so far. He thought of his grandmother, and of her way of teaching him just enough so he understood without letting him see the whole picture.

Sarah snorted, "Your family seems to have tons of secrets."

"Yeah...several are in my grandmother's grave." Sarah sat up and looked at him, clearly confused but he paid her no mind. "You mentioned dreams, Ivy. What would ghosts dream about?"

"They dream about tomorrow," she said. "Papa says they'll never see it, so they have to dream about it."

"And the wraiths?"

"Golden angels. He said they keep the dead asleep and if ever I'm in danger or I have to leave with nowhere to go, then I should look for them. Papa even taught me the secret password so they know I'm one of the good foals. I can't share it though," she said looking back at them. "I'm sorry."

"It's okay." Adrian said as he crouched low on the blanket. "Let's go. We'll going to visit my grandmother's barrow and see if the golden wraiths can help us."

Ivy's delighted whinny was his only warning before she threw herself into a headlong gallop. Through the trees and over trodden roads they raced. The only sound they could hear was the wind rushing by. Occasionally, Adrian would shout some direction to Ivy when the road forked ahead.

Despite their blinding speed, the sun still moved as they traversed the rocky roads. The sky bruised in reds, blues, and purples as the sun fell deeper and deeper behind the horizon. Adrian knew Lily would have loved the view.

Their path took them down into valleys, through the quiet farmlands and pastures of the Fultham lands. Past the pastures, however, they had to turn to rocky overgrown trails. It was one thing for the passing farming to see them, but too much closer to the Fultham home and seekers would be watching for those with significant connection to the Shom. Regardless of Sarah's magical aptitude, the presence of a shoshyuh and a familiar would incite immediate suspicion.

The less traveled roads were not as easy to navigate, even for Ivy. Careful of entangling her hooves, she slowed their pace to a canter. The trees that stretched around them hadn't been tended by any other hand but nature. Thorns, briars, and poison leaves lined the underbrush. The canopy was a tangled mess of living and dead branches. Even as they passed, a bough, just barely held by those around it, fell with a crash behind them.

Night had fallen by the time they came upon the solemn hills. Running like small mountains from north to south, each hill was adorned with a animal. It was the final burial of all direct descendants and all shoshyuh...or what was left of them.

One relic stood out from the others. Instead of a horse or rabbit or wolf, it held a winged woman with lions feet. That was the hill his grandmother had been buried, and so that was where they turned and continued their march.

"What is that?" Serah asked as they approached. "The Falwraiths have never had a winged shoshyuh."

He had asked the same question as a child. It was what the first matron wanted, his grandmother had said. Although, legend said the stone carver refused the first request, and the second had been modified.

The strange being's likeness appeared again on the door of the barrow, this time holding a sun and moon in each hand. Adrian frowned as the image struck a bell he could barely hear in his memory. Through the door, a hall of doors stretched before them only to vanish as the darkness became too great to see through. The majority of those doors were sealed, including the door who's metal plate had his grandmother's name etched on it.

"Alright," he said as he hopped off Ivy's back. "We'll rest here for the night."

"You can't be serious," Sarah said. "What is it with you and ghosts?"

"That was one time. Look, we need to rest and this is the safest place to do so." It was also the only place he thought he had the greatest chance of speaking to his grandmother's ghost, but he wasn't going to tell Sarah that.

"Well you can sleep in a crypt in you want. Ivy and I can sleep on top of the barrow." Sarah turned toward Ivy who was already getting comfortable on the ground.

Whatever look they exchanged, Ivy showed no interest in getting up from the earthen floor. With a huff, Sarah left, and the horse finished bedding down, asleep almost instantly.

Adrian turned back to his grandmother's tomb door. Curling up, he extended his mind into the Shom to find these ghosts that the mare said slept in the halls.

Every nook and cranny was laced with magic. It pulsed like the heartbeat of a slumbering giant. Adrian closed his eyes, letting the Shom guide his mind down silent halls and back again. Traces of the past lingered, overlapping in thin, fragile threads.

One thread, so faint that Adrian would have lost among the strong traces of spirits, was restless. The longer he focused, the more he could see the subtle beat with which it lashed about. Eyes shut tight, Adrian rose to his feet and began following the thread. Stone gave way to packed earth beneath his paws, then blades of grass cooled by the night air. Four more strands, equally frail and restless, met his path.

Down hall and over the grassy meadow between the barrows the strands led. Mists obscured his path. His friends, his ancestors, all he knew faded away in the mists. Cold, dew-covered stone pressed against his nose, and he jumped back eyes opening to see where he had been led. Far to his left and right, and stretching high above him, was the face of a cliff. Lines etched in iron and smoothed by time painted the surface with five ancient symbols and a sixth he had not seen—a sheep's head. It sat at the bottom, directly across from the twisting roots of the oak tree. All five of the strands led beyond the door, as if calling him to find a way inside this ancient, forgotten barrow.

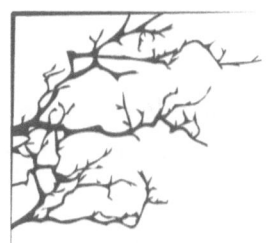

Chapter 5

"They called to you too, didn't they?" The voice, distorted by the veil of death, was unmistakable to the fox. He turned, tears stinging the corners of his vision as he beheld his grandmother's spirit. It was as if time had rewound, the lines of illness and the pallor of death no longer clutched at her so tightly. Her silver curls were long again, and swayed in a breeze Adrian could not feel. Her eyes were sharp, attentive, no longer glossed over with the strain of nightly fevers.

"You're whole again," Adrian said. In this form of his, the woman seemed taller than life, just as she had been in his early childhood.

"My mind is at least...and that mind of mine is sad to see the fate that has befallen my grandchildren."

"But you can fix it right? You knew the ancient magic better than anyone in our house. You have to know something to reverse this curse."

When she said nothing, his heart seemed to slide into a pit there was no escape from. Little did he know, the pit was much deeper than he knew.

"I...can't reverse it, can I?"

"Unfortunately not to my knowledge," With a sigh, she looked to the door. Her brow furrowed the way it used to when she beheld a loathsome problem. "I knew the moment your mother spoke with Catherine that the fate of both you and Lily were sealed."

Adrian's ears perked up. His hackles rose. He wanted to asked, needed to know what she meant, but he knew the answer would come if he waited and listened.

"It's time," she turned those piercing eyes on Adrian. "It's time you learned the true weight of the curse of the five houses. Sister's willing, this information may help you to escape your fate."

When next she spoke, her voice had become deep and soft with sadness. Adrian sat at her feet, watching the air around them shimmer with the lingering energy of the past. "At the end of the last kingdom, the royals were succeeded by six children, not the five that we had taught. When the War of Kings began, something had been awakened in the earth; it was something that simple magic and annual offerings could no longer contain."

"When the King and Queen were slain, you see, with them died the knowledge of how to contain it. Their children had not yet earned the knowledge, and so the children had to figure out for themselves how to save their kingdom from both the war and the terror that war had awoken. The ram on this gate, nearly erased by time, was the crest of the brother. It was he that paid the price to contain the terror, his sisters then paid the price to appease the King."

Adrian remembered the stories of the five sisters well. They gave up their throne to prevent the slaughter of their people. To maintain this peaceful solution, the first born of each of the five houses was given to serve the kingdom of Rohgrik as tribute. It was something that every successor of the houses were made to pay as a show of continued deference to the throne. His eldest sister was only fifteen when she was sent away. She would be well over twenty by the time she returned...if she ever did.

"The brother," his grandmother continued, "became the first shoshyuh. From the ram, came the oak tree—the same that the matron of the oak has kept for centuries."

"You make it sound like the matron has been alive for as long as the oak," Adrian observed.

"She has. She and all of the matrons, aside from your mother, have been around since the first shoshyuh was created. It's blood magic as old as magic itself. You see, Adrian, when the sister's unearthed the spell for the shoshyuh blessing, they also unearthed the means for immortality. The shoshyuh and familiars they produced all contain the raw energy of life. That energy, when harvested, can be converted into raw vitality."

"If all of that is true, why is our house so different?"

"We are different because it is a lot harder to say what you are doing is right, when it is a human that you are killing."

Adrian sat back on his heels. He wanted to shout that *he* was human, that all of the shoshyuh were human. But that same argument, those same words held the reason of the other houses. They *were* human, but not anymore. His body was that of a fox, all who saw him would only see him as such.

He looked down at his paws: the mud seeped between his furry toes staining the golden fur a dingy brown. He had no clue about the other houses. The Fulthams hadn't removed themselves from the darkness. They had allowed themselves to become blinded to it in favor of the candle they clutched to their chest. The Feyse saw it, and poisoned the candle to bring them back to heel—to remind them that they were anything but free.

"Our aunt, the Fultham Shoshyuh before Lily...and the others. Where...Are they still...?"

"Alive?" his grandmother supplied. "Only the one you know as your aunt. The one before her, my sister, I couldn't save. Before I wrestled power from the first Fultham matron, our shoshyuh were sacrificed much like the others. Once they produced the heirs and a new child was chosen for the role, their blood was spilled for the blessing, and their flesh was harvested for the feast. The only difference between how they were treated and how the other shoshyuh were treated was that the matrons did not consume much of the flesh—only enough to sustain themselves until the next blessing. What they did not consume went to the other shoshyuh, to strengthen them instead."

"Your mother's sister," she continued, "The woman who actually birthed you and Lily, I sent away. *Far* away and made it so that she seemed to have died of illness."

Adrian hung his head, a whimper escaping as the information beat down on him. There was both too much, yet not enough, and there was no time to digest. There was one line he understood, one thread of knowledge he could focus on:

"So there is nothing I can do except run? And hope I can find Lily when she's sent away?"

Sadness painted his grandmother's spectral face. He had made an assumption. The bite of fear sent a shudder down Adrian's spine. Surely it was not wrong that he could run. He could run now if only...

"Lily," he began, "Lily is going to be sent away right?"

His grandmother shook her spectral head. His mother, she explained, is not strong enough to go against the other matrons. His sister will be partnered with a nobleman and allowed to live until she births tribute, heir, and a replacement. It was never on him to continue the line. It was on him to care for the line and to make sure that the king and the houses were paid their dues.

Dawn broke through the mist as Adrian collapsed in the damp grass. Tears dampened his muzzle. He wanted to bury himself and the knowledge. He couldn't run knowing that his sister was slated for death. There had a way to save them both. Looking on the old door, his eyes once again fell on the ram's head—both the symbol of the brother and the first sacrifice.

"You have a plan?" His grandmother asked as he pushed himself to his feet.

"I have a direction," he said. "The brother became the Great Tree, correct? Perhaps I can ask him what to do."

She smiled in that sad and understanding way that she used to in life. Her form began to dissipate leaving behind a disembodied warning. "A wise path. The knowledge is stored in the acorns, and from the acorns bread and other foods can be made. Tread carefully, the tree is well guarded. Only the shoshyuh of Thula has been able to gather the seed"

"Then that's were I'll go."

That morning, they were off again, riding through the forest and valleys at impossible speeds. Ivy tossed her mane in exhilaration while Adrian and Sarah hung on for dear life. There wasn't room for talking on the way, and there had been surprisingly few questions before they had left. Ivy had been ready to go anywhere it seemed. Sarah, on the other hand, was more than willing to help in exchange for one of the acorns.

Huntson was average compared to the size of the other four cities. No river divided its residents, but broad, shallow streams lazed through pastures and farms. Those pastures, where animals trodded slowly about, was where Ivy left them. There were other things she wanted to see, and Adrian could call for her next he needed the mare's help. On foot, Sarah and he continued from the outer farms into the town proper.

Houses pressed so close even cats had difficulty using the alleys. Wells covered by little roofs and hanging cloths sprouted up from the cobble roads at every block. At the city's center, a gathering square paved in river stone and edged in grey brick was surrounded by shops and merchant wagons. A large marble fountain stood in center. Adrian was sure the fountain had been a thing of beauty before algae and filth turned the water into a murky cesspool of frogs and insects.

The crowning piece, a robed figure stood headless. The tilted vase that once poured water was clutched in cracked fingers and coated in blue slime. Like a steady drip, flakes of the slime tore away at the mouth of the vessel, and tumbled down the thin water fall into the pool.

Above it all, the family manor rose; it was a benevolent, withered giant that watched the sleepy buildings. Standing on the fountain, his fur darkened to avoid attention, Adrian could pick out the moss-covered cracks and missing shingles of the manor. The air of nobility seemed stale, long bled away through cracks and drafty windows.

Night fell, framing the manor in misty starlight. Golden feathers glimmered briefly on the second floor. The shoshyuh sang its lament to the wind. It was not allowed to fly free this night.

In the deepest hour of the moon, Adrian crept up to the hedges that lined the manor's yard. Sarah shuffled behind him, her dress pinned to her belt to avoid it catching on branches or thorns. All around them, magic pulsed in the air; the hedges, the wooden fences beyond, and the pebbled walkways through the garden all had a history that tied them to the Shom. The fence, a simple boundary, had been through several enchantments over the decades. From being an alert system, to a sheild, to a quiet alert once more, the wood was nearly widdled away by the runes and prayers scrawled over it's surface.

Adrian silenced the spell with on of his own, creating a gap in the parameter than he and Sarah could slip through. Before them, the garden stretched toward the manor. Up close it wasn't as large as Adrian thought. Two stories made up the core of the structure and attached to one corver was a stone tower that reached just a few feet higher than the rest of the building. It was from the tower that the bird's song came.

"Sarah," He said. "Avoid touching the paths and climb the window as quietly as you can. I'll use my spells to keep the house asleep while you retrieve the shoshyuh fur us to talk with. Ignore anything you might see. Pick up only the cage the golden bird is in and climb back out of the window."

She frowned, crossing her arms as he leaped over the fence. "Why can't you just lift me to the window? I don't have any way to keep from falling off the tower."

"The spell to keep everyone asleep is delicate. I can't both keep them asleep and get you into the tower."

She crept, unhappy and silent, across the wide field. He followed at her heels until he could sense everyone that spelt inside and guarded outside. Hidden in the tall grass, he gathered and wove the threads of magic, casting them over the house like a great quilt. By the time he saw Sarah vanish into the second-story window, every person on the property was under his spell.

Sarah winced, massaging her palms as she crouched beneath the window. If she only had magic, she could have just been lifted to the window. But no, she had to be born as some magickless freak in the Feyse house. The distinct lack of dust, feathers, or bird droppings improved her mood as she crept deeper into the little avery.

Feathers whispered and settled to her left. In the starlight, little bird cages sat together: silver, wooden, golden, each decorated with wire vines and glass leaves. Behind them all was a large cloth dome. Another shuffle. A soft whistle of a sigh. It was the only cage that had a cover, and all the others held little yellow and black birds that were sound asleep.

Sarah reached for the cage, carefully lifting it up and over the smaller cages. The wooden frame creaked in complaint. Its occupant shuffled again but did not make a sound otherwise. She turned to go, having fixed the cage to her hip, when she saw the small glint of gold beneath the table.

Acorns, golden with the life power of the Great Tree, sat piled in a wicker basket. Nearly a dozen were there, all round as if they had just been plucked from the tree. Sarah knew the legends, the knowledge those fruits could impart. She could take two, one for the fox and one for herself. Then both of their questions could be answered, and she could go home.

The bird didn't approve of this. The moment she lifted an acorn from the basket, it let out a shriek that left her ears ringing. Sarah would have wrung its neck if it wasn't needed alive...and if the guards didn't immediately charge through the unlocked door.

When Sarah was guided out of her little windowless bedroom hours later, the first thing she noticed was vines. Every wall was covered in their trailing paths. Huge green leaves and delicate blue morning glories hid the cracks and flaws their roots had caused. The next thing Sarah noticed was the floor as she tripped. A section of wood had come loose, the corner held just high enough by a root to catch unaware feet.

A rough hand caught her before she fell on the malicious root. Then she was on her feet again, her arm aching from the gaurd's grip as she was ushered along. Like the Feyse mansion, paintings and tapestries hung on every wall; but unlike home, the decorations of House Thula had to content with wild growth. Everything woven had more than one hole due to moths or wayward roots.

The meeting chamber was not much different than the halls. The leaves were wilted, the roots thicker, and the spiraling trunk of a tree jutted through floor and ceiling. Below the canopy the high seat sat, and above the branches were filled with birds of prey. Their gleaming talons left sap filled welts on their perches.

In the high seat, the matron of the house sat, her frail, withered form nothing like the youthful glow she wore outside. Sarah almost didn't recognize her until the woman spoke:

"The Fasye brat? Really...Catherine wasn't satisfied ruining the Fulthams and had to come after me as well?"

Sarah pulled her lips into a thin line. If she said too much or not enough, she'd be sent home. Possibly to endure much worse punishment for betraying the family than the fox.

Matron Thula shook her head in dismay, "Did you think I wouldn't recognize you? You're the spitting image of your mother, her soul rest with the sisters."

Sarah's shoulders jerked back. Thula broke out laughing.

"Oh!" The crone wiped her eyes with the back of her hand. "She seriously thought to keep the wool over our heads? The old bat can take that as payment for the rude visit to my shoshyuh."

"I don't...what are you talking about? My mother gave me to House Feyse to serve the shoshyuh."

"Your mother didn't give you away! You were born a slave. Born from the very shoshyuh you were told to tend."

She took a step back, the room lurching beneath her even as the gloved hands of the guards steadied her. The laughter only grew, becoming a cackling screech that summoned the calls of the watching falcons and hawks. Sarah covered her ears, trying to think through the deceit of the matron.

But it wasn't deceit. It was just the painful truth.

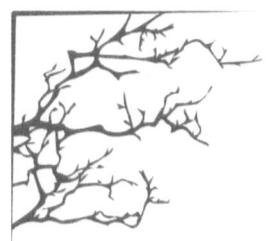

Chapter 6

Golden fur that covered a scared body and framed gentle amber eyes. Those eyes were enraged at every glance and mention of her matron. The bear and the wolf. Both hated the matron but for her they would relax. Both would curl around her and let her lay against their fur in the gardens. She had known it was her father that was called to become the wolf, but the bear...she didn't know. Or she thought she didn't know.

Out of the cackles and screeching calls around her, a woman's somber voice recited the Cycle of the Houses:

"Blood thrice spilt for freedom-
King, prince, pawn.
Now thrice it must be spilt once more:
Once for the king, who taxes our life,
Once for the Shom, who taxes our soul,
And the last for the house, who's tax
Is for food, for safety, and power."

The golden bird circled overhead before perching between two hawks that dwarfed the little songbird. Sarah glared at the bird. Adrian could have at least warned her the bird was loyal to its house.

"This is my shoshyuh," Matron Thula said. "Pretty little thing, no? I was so happy when she kept her voice. It lets her tell me so many things after her nightly adventures. Things like a golden bear birthing a human baby. Or a little gold fox that runs with the horses." The crone smiled then, and Sarah's skin writhed.

"You let your shoshyuh roam free?"

"Sometimes," Thula said coyly. "Other times I keep her in one of her pretty cages so she can sing to me. You see, dear, I don't treat my descendants near as poorly as Catherine does. You could say I like to move where the wind takes me, so then I can take advantage of any tools that happen across my path."

"What are you planning to do to me?"

"To you?" Thula laughed. "Oh dear, I'm not going to do anything to you. If your matron wants to play, I'll be more than happy to join the game."

Sarah's confusion only served as encouragement to the elder.

"I'll give you my shoshyuh. She's a ripe bird, three generations old due to a bought of barren wombs my line seems afflicted with. Oh, don't look so skeptical, I'll only give her to you if you bring me the shoshyuh of House Huve. The horse must be alive, and it must be mature. And I know it will be, provided that loon doesn't bend to Catherine's most recent bought of insanity."

Sarah shuddered. She could smell with metallic tinge of blood again. She clenched her fists, focusing on the sting of her nails in her palms. So focused was she that she didn't hear the crone's next orders. Mutely, she followed the promptings of the guards. Out of the room and down the hall, she stepped without being there. Her mind was somewhere else...somewhere dark.

The room was dark, but far from silent as Adrian padded beneath the tables and chairs. To call it an aviary was an insult to bird keeping, but that's what it was intended as. Cages, some wood, others copper, iron, or gold, were scattered about every available surface that wasn't on the floor. A few were empty, others contained anywhere from one to three songbirds. Each was a different color, but all had golden accents on their throats and bellies.

"Shoshyuh," one of them whispered. It was a little cardinal, the gold out of place amongst her brown feathers. "Shoshyuh."

He did his best to shoosh the little bird, fearful her shrill voice would bring the guards. None came, and still the little bird called for him to come near.

"Help us shoshyuh," it said. "We do not like these cages, and our mother cannot break the locks."

"Who is your mother?" The locks were little more than wire wrapped around the doors and twisted on itself. Nothing for a human to undo, but for an animal it would be easier to break the cage.

"A shoshyuh," it chirped.

"Like you," another said.

Adrian furrowed his brow. These were all familiars, just like the badger and ivy. Perhaps the Thula Shoshyuh had taken to collecting songbirds and imbuing them with magic. It didn't seem like that far of a stretch considering how shoshyuhs are made.

"Help us," the cardinal cried again, the others repeating like a small chant.

"Help us."

"Help us."

"We want to see the sky."

"We don't want to go through the door."

"Help us."

Adrian stepped back, his ears falling against the back of his skull as the chant grew more frantic. Boots fell on the wooden floor outside, the battered floor groaning with protest. He dove beneath the nearest item, a wicker basket that had been overturned. His foot touched something small and round but his attention was on the door as it opened.

A guard's voice demanded quiet before shutting the door again. Wings flapped overhead. The familiars hushed; their beaks turned upward to follow the newcomer's flight. For one beat, then two, Adrian held his breath. Thula's falcons were legendary for their brutality; if one had come, it would be impossible to escape unharmed.

Claws, delicate and tiny, landed on the handle of his basket. The presence of the shoshyuh pulsed like a heartbeat against the Shom. Though it pulsed quickly, feeding the air with anxious energy, there was a purpose to it.

"Shoshyuh," the bird chirped. "I'd like to know the meaning of your visit. Be truthful or I will make sure your little thief does not make it out of the city."

Adrian curled up tighter beneath the basket, the smell of other, more powerful birds grew stronger in the room. "I...we were trying to rescue you. We need information-"

"You wanted the acorns then." The tiny claws vanished as she hopped away. The basket disappeared next, knocked away by a large dark feathered falcon.

Scrambling back, he wasn't fast enough to avoid the sharp claws that came for him. He hit the floor, pinned at the neck by claws more powerful than he thought possible for such a bird. Adrian closed his eyes, sending a silent apology to his sister.

The killing move didn't come.

Those delicate feet landed on his shoulder, behind the powerful leg that trapped him. "I almost pity you. The Fesyes are known to be cruel to their shoshyuh."

"But that's why I left."

The golden songbird tilted her head to one side, then the other. All attention was on her, the tension coiling around her forming decision. At last, she gave a sign, the ruffling and smoothing of her shining feathers. The grip released, allowing air come more freely to him.

When he didn't move, she flitted to the overturned basket. "I believe in your intentions, but I cannot go with you."

"Why? The windows aren't locked, and you've been able to fly as far as the neighboring city." Adrian shifted to lay more comfortably on the floor, shielding his vulnerable underside from further threats.

With a sigh, she looked toward the caged chicks. Their beady little eyes watched her with veneration and a deep respect. She only shook her head. "I must perform my duty. The Matron must be fed."

Recognition, with its horrid clarity, jolted Adrian. "The familiars...they're yours?"

"You should leave. Whatever your questions are, seek the heart of it at the Lake of the Thousand Souls. I will give you the offering to summon the ancient naiad, but that is all I can do."

Whistling to another of her guards, she directed a small satchel to be gathered. Into it three golden acorns were placed along with a scroll case containing a map and notes. He sat quietly, watching the birds flit about as they followed her command without a call between them.

Leaving the packing to her retinue, the songbird flitted to the filled cages. Her whispers were too quiet for him to hear, but he could see the inhabitants settled onto their perches. Within moments many of them were tucking their heads into their wings for sleep.

Adrians harness shifted as the parcel was tucked into a side pocket. He snorted in mild relief. It was a pocket he could easily reach—opposite from the journal. No words were exchanged as he slipped back onto the window ledge, only a shared glance between a tired elder and a determined youth. Then he was gone.

He found Sarah waiting for him on the road, her face and clothes clean, and her bag heavy on her back. Silence deadened the air as she fell in step with his easy trot. Her air was troubled, her step so low as to almost be a shuffle. At the first cross roads he slowed his step, watching as she hesitated before turning toward the eastern path.

When he didn't follow, her shoulders slumped farther, the indecision fading to annoyance. "Why did you stop?"

"What happened between you and Matron Thula?"

"Does that matter to you? Your neck wasn't on the chopping block back there. Hey, where are you going?"

Adrian trotted quietly into the forest, off the path. If Sarah wanted to keep secrets, he could continue the search with out her. Unfortunately, she wasn't as willing to part ways. Her steps, clumsy from surprise, followed him.

The woodland underbrush soon thickened, requiring him to jump or crawl to proceed. Vines that hardly troubled his

agile paws, became hazardous for her boots, making her trip
and stumble through bushes he had just passed beneath. After
the first few hours, Sarah ceased to call for him. After the first
day, she ceased speaking at all.

That night he heard her collapse, a soft, crackling thud
against the leaf strewn ground. Turning back, he saw her pull
herself up and curl against the base of a tree. Pitying the lifeless
look in her eyes, he showed himself only long enough to give
her the comfort of a small fire. A glimmer of hope was all he
received.

Crisp morning air greeted them followed by the fog that
waited outside their tent. The smell of lake water, soured fish
and sodden mud grew to become a constant companion by
that afternoon. Fog caressed their heels until the evening hour
when they again stopped to rest. It was just after the moon
graced the sky with light that soft blue wisps of light appeared.
Dancing and bobbing between the trees, Adrian couldn't help
but notice the silver threads that trailed around the specters.
The spiraled in the wind, framing each ghostly faerie in a
twisting halo of magic.

The wisps were common enough in the kingdom; they
gathered wherever the Shom was the most potent. The trails
of energy, however, had only been mentioned in dusty tombs.
Each strand was pure, unaltered magic, shaped and animated
by the living energies of the land. It was the magic of the trees,
the wind, and the earth. They must have been getting close to
the lake as the whisps seemed as numerous as the stars.

Watching the procession pass them by, Adrian could feel
a strong pull towards the threads. It was as if they were apart
of him, or he some extension of them. Each night they stayed

in the forest, he felt a pull from the procession. The sway and pulse of wild shome called to him. His breathing slowed. His heart seemed to time to their beat.

But he couldn't follow. To follow a whisp, even for a shoshyuh, risked losing oneself to the lull of the Shom.

The path only grew more wild with each day. Vines grew thorns, and the trails of woodland creatures grew scarce. The elms that he had scarcely noticed before, now stood out with darkened, peeling bark. The oaks vanished, and black birches grew in their place branches clawing at the sky for the last shreds of light.

There came a night where both the moon and stars were obscured by heavy clouds. The earthy smell of rain was thick in the air. Adrian slowed his advance, wary of the predators he sensed in the shadows. That night, he did not let Sarah sleep alone beneath a tree but sat beside her. With a small pulse of magic, he was able to feel the thorny vines that lay around them. It only took a small push to draw them in and up. The woven tent they became wouldn't stand up against a determined bear, but it might convince a wolf or forest cat to look elsewhere for food.

Sarah opened her pack and pulled out some bread and cheese, these she split between them with a little sausage added to his plate. Her voice was barely a whisper when she asked what had lightly plagued her from the start of their departure:

"You left me..."

"Our goals no longer aligned." Adrian took a bite of the bread, it was still soft despite their time on the road. "Why did you follow me?"

She chewed on her food in silence, staring at the tiny flames of Adrian's fire. It wasn't much, but it was warm. Finally, she spoke. "I have no where else to go. Catherine would kill me if I returned and I can't do Thula's task without you...she agreed to give me her shoshyuh if I got her the shoshyuh of House Huve."

"I have no interest in kidnapping shoshyuh."

"But if we have them, we could free them, right? Found a way to help them escape so they wouldn't be harvested..."

"The five houses would just make new shoshyuh."

Sarah threw her hands up before tearing another piece from her food. Adrian sighed, and looked out at the wisps that bobbed along outside. The ghostly blue lights were the only illumination, and they seemed unbothered as a gust of wind whistled through the trees and bushes.

"Why are you so bent on releasing the shoshyuh?"

She didn't answer.

He didn't press, simply called for a curtain of leaves between them, and set down to read before sleep.

"My father," Her voice was so soft, he would have missed it had he still been human, "he was the last Feyse shoshyuh. ."

Adrian's ears pricked up. Slowly, he turned to look at her through the vines.

"I never knew my mother," Sarah continued. "According to Sandra...she was the shoshyuh before him."

"The Bear? But if that were true, you would be the heir."

"An heir with no ability for magic, useless for spells or reagents, and unable to birth a successor...a shame worth hiding I suppose."

Rage, quiet and sharp, simmered in his chest. He was reminded all over again of the little birds with their gold markings—children waiting for slaughter. Had Sarah been one such child? Had Lily? Behind closed doors while he had been studying, he had no knowledge of happened to his twin. The wind picked up, whistling through the branches as it reacted to his connection to the Shom.

Sarah edged back from him, her back pressing against the vine walls of their tent. "Adrian?"

Adrian was silent. He wrestled his breathing into a slower rhythm. Worry for his family, his sister, threatened to consume him. They had no heir. His sister was expected to provide but had no suitors. She was alone with people that could not understand her signs and motions...who could feign ignorance to obvious signs of displeasure. The pages of the journal began to flip and turn in rapid succession. Words and images glowed and flashed over the book, but he couldn't read any of it through the panic that gripped his mind.

But then it stopped. The air, the book, even the vines that made the tent went still. He blinked. A silvery blue wisp had appeared in the mouth of the tent..

As it slowly spiraled, the beat of his heart slowed. A single thread of light reached for him. Adrian leaned forward allowing the thread to alight on his nose before the world faded away into complete darkness. Sarah's cry preceded the silence that came next.

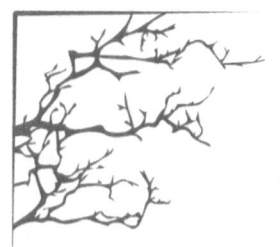

Chapter 7

The cold lake-side breeze roused Adrian from his stupor. The forest that surrounded him was gone. In its place was the edge of a short cliff that overlooked a lake. The water glowed with a silvery light. Mist danced over the waves, obscuring figures that appeared and disappeared like pale ghosts. They were the watchers, the thousand souls of all those that had died in a clash of power forgotten to history.

Wisps danced overhead in a sea of orbs. Up and down. Right and left. Each one moving in time with the next to form a rolling sea of light that wove the threads of Shom together. The watchers took the Shom from them and fed it into the mist and waters. Sarah gasped as she sat up beside him. "Where are we?"

"The Lake of a Thousand Souls..."

"She hungers," the sea whispered. "She craves."

The ground trembled, the vibration so subtle he wasn't sure it was real. Then it came again. The water's glow dimmed and surged outward in a pulse that reached as far as the shore. His chest tightened choking the breath from him. Instinctively, Adrian lowered his ears and pressed his belly against the ground.

A hand, slender and pale
rose from the waves; nails,
red as spilt blood, clawed

at magic above. Stole
the light for another moon
of life.

The threads of Shom lashed out as each one was drawn toward that hand. Writhing and twisting, each thread dissolved into the pale flesh. The wisps fled toward the edges of the lake, but one was too weak. Its screamed as it was pulled back, silenced once it met the naiad's hand.

Adrian panted. His claws dug into the soft soil as he was pulled toward the edge of the cliff. A portion of his magic was pulled into a single golden strand and broken free to feed the spirit of the lake.

But then it was done. The lights were reduced to a scattered handful of wisps that lingered at the shore. A woman as large as the ancient aspens that framed her domain, sat on the lake's surface. Her translucent face seemed somber as she met Adrian's gaze. She leaned toward him, reaching for the ledge that she stood on. With a yip he umped back, but could not escape. Held in the massive palm, dwarfed by the fingers that formed his new cage he trembled before the ancient naiad.

Her voice came as the drizzle of a spring rain, and the babble of a shallow brook: "You are so young... less than a moon."

He trembled, curling tight on himself as he gazed into eyes so dark they seemed black in the starlight.

"You have a soul that is both divided, and conflicted...how? Perhaps your other half is...no. I sense fear from that half, but no conflict."

"My other half?" Adrian's ears perked up. "My twin sister?"

"Ah," the nymph nodded. "A soul cleaved in the womb. A great duty must have demanded such an event."

He nearly asked the nymph what she was talking about and then shook his head. This wasn't what he came here for. He looked back, where Sarah still cowered on the edge of the cliff. A touch on his mind, chilled as a mountain stream, sent a shiver up his spine.

"You're curiosity burns," the nymph mused. "But you do not ask...why?"

"I have a different question, one I sought you for."

"Ah...you have helped to feed me this moonless night, so I will answer this question. Ask it thoroughly, as I will answer only the one without further tribute."

"How do I reverse the shoshyuh blessing? I want to return to my normal self, before I was forced to undergo the ritual."

"Ah...clarity comes to every stream in time," she said. "Listen carefully, as it will be on your heart to remember and to understand what I tell you this night:

"To become a shoshyuh, blood must be spilt to allow room for the Shom. Time must then be allowed for the flesh and the soul to mend. In five years, it will be as if it always was, and to remove the Shom will be as if removing the heart.

For your soul, half shoshyuh, half conflicted, you have less time. Three months, and your form will be permanent."

"But how can I reverse it?" he pleaded.

She shook her head, eyes welling with an emotion he could not place. "Blood was spilled to bind the Shom, so blood must be spilled to release it. The chains were forged by the desires of those that made you, so they must be sundered by desires as strong and pure. Before your third night beneath the light of the invisible moon you must:

> *Free the souls bound*
> *By blood and greed.*
> *By their hands pierce*
> *The heart, remove*
> *The head, severe*
> *The paws.*

"This sacrifice will be great, and the toll will be high for whichever path you take. The first will free you, and leave the others bound, the second will devour you to break the chains of others. In the end, the choice has to be yours, and it must be free of doubt."

Adrian paled, the starlit sky and those deep eyes beginning to spin as his heart raced. Death, it seemed, was his only escape. He sought the ancient gaze for more answers, for comfort, but her voice only echoed in his head.

Two months left. Death to reverse the spell, or death to fuel the conflict between houses. He shook his head as the nymph lowered him back to the cliff face.

"Thank you," he whispered to her. Landing beside his companion, he turned and gave the nymph a deep bow.

She nodded, her smile both pleased and somber. Then her attention turned to Sarah who had risen to shaking feet.

"Great spirit," Sarah said. "I call for your knowledge. Accept this gift in exchange for the answers I seek." With the songbird's scroll in one hand, she cast the acorns to the nymph with the other.

The three acorns stopped to hover in the air, their golden light faded, replaced by a silvery sheen the nymph pulled away and consumed. The seeds, devoid of magic and life, fell to the ground. The nymph sighed as the magic helped to sate her hunger:

"I accept the sacrifice made on your behalf. Three seeds, three lives that can no longer be, and three questions I will answer."

"Who was the woman who birthed me? What happened to her?"

The spirit's brows furrowed, her eyes turning to the stars, as if searching for the answers before returning to the tiny human before her. "Alice, the second of her generation, fulfilled the duties as an heir before she was called to fill the role of Shoshyuh. Six moons before your birth, she was made to fill the calling. A bear she became, a human she birthed, and a bear she died."

Sarah trembled, her voice rough as it grew louder. "What am I?"

"The same as the shoshyuh, but also the same as the ones you call familiars. Your shackles bind you, not to control as they do others, but to protect."

"What do you mean by that?"

However, the naiad was done. With one last glance glance to Adrian, the spirit of the lake turned and sank back into the lake's depths. With a curse, Sarah kicked the lifeless apple seeds over the cliff.

"Call her back," she said. In his silence, she turned on him. "I said call her back. You gave her something, give her more!"

Adrian shook his head, retreating back into the forest. "I don't have much more to give. I have my answers and you have yours. Its time to rest and think so we can act."

"So that's it?" Her earlier trepidation apparently forgotten as she stormed after him. "You have two months left to live and I still don't know what's wrong with me?"

"I got the information I needed."

"And I didn't. So help me call her back."

Adrian sighed. The fatigue was eating at him now, and he wanted—*needed*—to rest. He wasn't really sure why Sarah was still following him anyway. The days since his escape had blended together so thoroughly he hadn't even thought about it.

By smell alone he found their camp. The tent was as they had left it, as was Sarah's ration bag. Beneath the relative protection of the twisted vines, Adrian turned to Sarah.

"None of this is going to work if our goals conflict."

"That's rich," she said. "You have no idea what life has been like as the abandoned brat of the Feyse house. And now I find that not only were both of my parents harvested by that crazy woman, but that I'm cursed?"

Adrian leaned back, ears flat against his head as Sarah paced back and forth in front of the tent. "That doesn't change that our goals have to align if we are to work together."

"Work together to do what?! To run away? To kill you so maybe you come back as a human? What are you going to do as a human? The houses will still be the same festering disease they've always been and I'll...I'll still be a mistake."

Sarah trembled as she sunk to the ground outside of the tent. He crept forward as she buried her head in her arms, hugging her knees tight to her chest.

"My entire life," she continued in a hoarse voice. "I believed my mother had abandoned me, that there was something so wrong that she left my dad and I behind with that horrible woman. The things I had to do to make up for that, to try and be good enough for my mother to come back and save me...they will haunt me until I've rotted to nothing but bones."

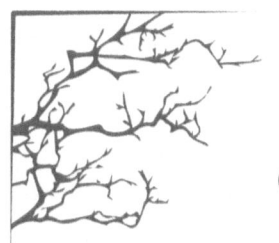

Chapter 8

The uneasy silence that followed tainted Adrian's sleep with nightmares of bears and wolves. The morning, punctuated by a light drizzle of rain, felt tainted as they made their way back to the roads in silence. In a round about way, Sarah had made a point: they had no goal now.

So while they waited on the roadside for Ivy to come to his call, Adrian allowed the problem turn around and around in his mind. He knew running was not an option; Lily would be left to die by their mother's hand. Could he really protect her on his own whether in human form or not? He wasn't so sure.

He wanted more information, and Sarah had made an agreement that would allow them to get close access to the shoshyuh of house Thula again. Ivy, apparently familiar with the home of House Huve, pranced about in circles once she found they were going to visit the horse shoshyuh. Sarah had barely settled on her back behind Adrian before the mare was off at a gallop over the roads.

The horse, the symbolic animal of work and health, had powers unique to its position. It's magic revolved around speed and resources. The cropland surrounding Riverton amply showed this in the plump greenery with orange, yellow, and green fruits ripe more than two weeks into the season. With the river having run dry generations ago, Adrian wasn't sure the town would survive without the shoshyuh.

No one gave them a second glance as Ivy left them in a cloister of trees outside the town gates. Into crowded streets Adrian and Sarah walked, the former dulling his fur to look more like a stray dog than a fox. At the earliest opening n the forest of legs and skirts, Adrian slipped into Riverton's alleyways.

"We need to find where the shoshyuh of the Huve is housed," he said as Sarah took a seat nearby. "You should find lodging and figure out what all this excitement is about."

Sarah nodded, eyeing the crowd as she kept her voice low. "It's a celebration of some kind. At the very least it can offer us some cover when we leave with the shoshyuh."

He cocked his head to give her a dubious look. "You're still wanting to trade him?"

"No," she said, "But there's a chance he isn't as keen on staying as the bird was. I heard there will be a blessing ceremony soon."

"A blessing ceremony," he said, "so he may be in danger?"

"It's a possibility."

"Thula is breeding her shoshyuh for food. Huve hasn't changed shoshyuh in multiple generations, I wonder if she is also breeding her shoshyuh for an alternative harvest." That seemed to make her stop, her wide eyes searching for something in his face. He sighed, realizing Thula hadn't told Sarah much of what she uses Shoshyuh for.

"Thula learned that breeding a shoshyuh produces familiars. And she's been consuming them for power instead of risking the continuation of her bloodline. If that plan has been working so well for her, why the sudden interest in change? She can't seriously be thinking of changing her tactic now just because you visited her shoshyuh."

"She thinks Catherine is up to another one of her games."

"It still doesn't feel like we can see the entire picture. Walk and mingle around, see what gossip you can pick up and then meet me at the inn by the city center."

It was evening before Sarah finally stopping mingling to find a place to sleep for the evening. In the room the innkeeper had selected, curled up on the bed, Adrian sat curled up asleep. He was up immediately as the door was opened and peered at Sarah between beady eyes. With a yawn, he stretched and sat up to fill her in on his plan.

"I thought you weren't going to help with this?" She said after he had finished.

"We're just going to talk to him and then let him chose his own way."

There was darkness behind her surprised look as he curled up on the bed. It didn't linger, making him question if it had actually been there. "This plan uses the same rules as last time right?" she asked. "I slip in, saddle the horse-"

"No saddle, it's too risky. Just let him out in whatever the stable boy left him in when the spell activates."

"You can't be serious."

He didn't answer, instead watching her as the end of his tail flicked against the soft comforter. With a frustrated sigh she pushed him off the bed. "Fine. I'm not staying up all night though, go rest on a windowsill and wake me when its time."

With a small huff, he jumped into the lone chair in the room and watched the street through the shutters. It was quiet, a little too quiet for a celebratory night. He tried not to let that bother him as he counted down the hours.

In the pre-dawn light, he pulled and coaxed the Shom into himself. The power shifted to his will. It was easier than the first time, though he was still restricted in how far he could throw the spell around them. He felt little specks of power, souls of servants, guests, and guards. Most were asleep. Some, however, were still awake. Those he concentrated his spell around, easing them into a light slumber.

Five souls whose light shone twice that of the others were in the house. They were the matrons. Four slumbered soundly, the fifth roamed the gardens. All five he left alone, unwilling to risk alerting them should they be sensitive to his magic. Once the magic had settled into place, Adrian focused again on the world he could see.

Sarah's hands ached as she gripped the fence. Finally, the fox opened his eyes and gave her a slight nod. Mercifully, jumping a fence was much easier than climbing a tower...until she landed in a dried pile of dung. The smell made her eyes sting and followed her as she left the fence, and the fox, behind.

The stable loomed ahead. The gray planks were dotted with holes that were filled with a black maud. The roof, at least, had been properly patched leaving the inside dry—or as dry as it could be.

Snoring in the corner, covered in what she could only guess was beer, was the stable hand. His fingers were gripped tight around a lead that disappeared over a stable door. Placing one foot in front of the other as slowly as she could, Sarah peeked into each of the six stables, hoping her quarry wasn't what the stable boy clung to in his sleep.

The first two sables were empty. The third held a sleeping guard that had lost his helmet somewhere between his last post and wherever he found the bottle of wine that had spilled on the straw beside him. The fourth was empty again, though it had not been cleaned from its last guest.

Sarah pulled away from the stall door, leaving the guard to sleep soundly. With a few careful steps she was at the final stall. She peaked inside her breath catching in her throat as she met the large dark eyes of the Huve shoshyuh.

Those eyes froze her in place her with their raw intensity. Without light, they seemed almost black, but she could see the flecks of light that would make them a deep amber in the daylight. Unable to hold his stare, her eyes drifted to his golden coat, and the bits of carved bone braided into his long, silken mane. With a flex of his powerful chest and leg he stomped a hoof as if demanding to know her business.

Sweat beaded on the back of her neck. The horse was massive, sixteen hands tall at the least, yet she had been unable to see it until she had opened the door. Now, with it staring down on her, she became all too aware of her smaller stature. When she failed to speak, the horse craned its head closer, ears flat against his neck.

"You shouldn't be here," the stallion said. "Leave before I break whatever spell you paid for."

She suppressed a shiver, feeling the blood leave her cheeks. "I-We can to free you."

"I doubt it."

"No...really. I want to help you get out of here. You're slated to be harvested, right? That's why everyone is celebrating outside."

The stallion's eyes narrowed, his forward hoof tearing into the ground in agitation. "I won't ask how you came by such knowledge and I also won't tell you again, Cursed One."

Sarah straightened herself immediately. With a silent snarl she grabbed his lead and pulled: "I'm trying to help you! Who are you to call me a cursed when you're sitting on death's row?!"

He jerked back, pulling her off her feet into his stall. His hoof tore at the ground, pulling up lines of golden thread before stomping them back into the dirt. Then, he brought his head down low whispering to her even as the stable-hand and guard began to rouse themselves: "Everything about you screams anger and pride. You are owed nothing, but demand I follow and obey? Count your blessing that I respect Alice too much to end your life."

The mention of her mother's name startled her. Even as she was hauled to her feet, she couldn't find any words to say or any strength to resist. All she could do was watch those eyes as they followed her removal from the stables.

Adrian flinched as his spell was ripped apart. Stars filled his vision, and he tried to shake them away. When that made the grass and sky sway and twist, he laid down. Spells had been broken before, his spells and the spells of others that had been cast on him, but the recoil had never hit him this hard before. He tried to regain his bearings. He could still see the stables as well as a guard pulling Sarah away.

He could do nothing for her. Not while each and every soul on the property was now stirring. The spell had been broken with so much force that everyone sensitive to the Shom felt it. He huddled down, letting the grass cover him. One of the souls he sensed was coming near. It must have been the one that had been in the gardens.

The soul did not veer away. It was walked towards him. One step after the other, it neared and he was left to either run and risk being seen, or hide and hope the powerful soul passed him.

"Adrian," came a whispered croak. "Where have you been, my little vixen?"

Catherine had found him.

The ground trembled with magic beneath his paws and he dashed away from the deranged elder. He needed to get away. He would help Sarah, but right now he had to escape.

"Oh you nasty little fox," the matron giggled. "Your tricks won't help you this time."

Catherine's blood-lust was palpable as it soak into the shadows that surrounded Adrian's flight. Pinpricks of red light appeared between the blades of grass growing and rising to follow on his heels. Jaws lined with sharp teeth snapped in the air behind him. They were too close. His tail and eyes stung as a tuft of fur was pulled free from his tail. His pursuers where silent, unnaturally so. Logically he knew he had to banish the spell. But the jaws. The jaws were too close, each snap removing just a little more fur from his tail and flank.

Mocking laughter followed him as he turned and dove for the fence. There was more than enough room for him, he already knew. What he hoped was that the fence would slow his pursuit, or allow him to get out of range of Catherine's shadow beasts. Eyes, red and glowing with hunger blinked at him beneath the fence. Adrian couldn't stop in time, and couldn't turn before the shadow hound lunged for him.

"Your line has a very nasty habit of disobedience," Catherine said. "First your matron, then your grandmother, and now you. It was a blessing that I was able to bring your current matron under heel."

Teeth, sharp and firm, pressed hard around Adrian's throat as he was drug before the woman. He didn't dare struggle, he could barely breath as it was. Catherine giggled, clapping her hands together as he was held down at her feet.

"I suppose I shouldn't complain. It's far too satisfying to crush that frivolous spirit. What difference does it make if I have to use force or threats?" Her wrinkled face and malicious eyes filled Adrian's vision as she kneeled in the tall grass. "I just wish I had gotten to your grandmother before the wasting took her. I had a very special plan for that little pest. I guess you'll just have to fill her place."

She took a knife from her belt, the sharpened steel glinted in the starlight. "Before that, there's a certain cub I need you to help me with." The vice grip of the wolf's jaw eased, allowing him to breath. The matron's hand ran through his fur, gentle as she surveyed his still form. Her voice came an awed whisper. "How beautiful you are. How perfect."

Her hand trailed over his nose and head before stroking his ear. His eyes grew heavy as she continued to pet his ear and whisper meaningless babbles to him. He knew she was using magic. He also knew there was nothing he could do. Agony cleared his mind as it exploded across the side of his head. He screamed, and thrashed against the maws that held him. At once his captors had him pinned once more to the ground, and through his blurred vision he could just barely make out the golden fox ear Catherine held in her hand.

She stared at it in wonder. As if consumed by thirst, her eyes glazed over and she brought the flesh to her lips to suckle the bleeding edge.

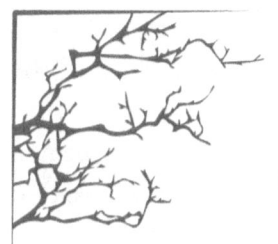

Chapter 9

Well after noon, the servants came to take her from the room she had been locked in. There had been ample time for the fox to come for her, but much like Thula's house, he was nowhere to be seen. She wasn't sure she could talk her way out of this, she hadn't even talked her way out of the last situation. Thula's whims had given her a deal for freedom.

Perhaps she could strike a deal with Matron Huve as well. As long as the other heads had not arrived yet, she had a chance to spin some tale about the other houses wanting to cause a little chaos. That chance, however, wasn't as available as she had hoped.

Sandra Huve, a thin woman with crisscrossing scars barely hidden beneath her lacy sleeves, was accompanied by the Matron Marianne Fultham. Sarah's confidence was gone. At any minute she could simply be killed and written off as a casualty of the celebration. Sandra's frown didn't help her outlook.

"Aren't you one of Catherine's pets?" She turned to Adrian's mother and repeated the question.

Marianne Fultham turned her empty gaze on Sarah. There was no emotion, no glimmer of humanity in her voice. "Yes, she was one of the house servants."

"Well?" Huve demanded of her. "Why'd you try to steal my horse? Catherine already eat Mary's kid? Damned glutton," she muttered, "going through three shoshyuh in one generation."

"I..." She trembled. Those golden eyes of Marianne seemed to burrow into her. Empty but demanding. Had they looked so haunted when they last met? She hadn't thought so.

Her life hadn't been the woman's hands back then either.

"Please," Sarah began. "I-I'm sorry. I didn't –"

The doors cracked open behind her. Huve cried out impatiently to the new arrival: "Catherine! Why'd your pet try to steal my horse?"

Slowly, praying Huve had mistaken the visitor, Sarah looked back. Eyes flat and dark as coal met her gaze. She hadn't been mistaken.

"Sarah," her grandmother said, the chill of disappointment dripped from her voice. "Is this what you've been up too? Bringing shame to the House that took you in as a squalling infant?"

Sarah opened her mouth to speak, but couldn't find any word except one. "Matron?"

"You dug your own grave," Catherine snapped, joining the other women.

Adrian's mother arched a thin eyebrow, glancing between the two. A flicker of something disturbed her hazel eyes but was gone as soon as it had appeared.

Sandra clapped her hands, almost bouncing on her toes. "Oh goody, you weren't after my horse, Catherine. I was terribly upset, especially after I offered to share him at the feast. Oh! You said 'grave' does that mean you wouldn't mind if I..."

She looked meaningfully between Sarah and Matron Feyse, a shy smile twisted her thin lips.

A weight, as heavy as the largest river stone, settled on Sarah's shoulders as her grandmother inclined her head to Huve. "Continue as you would, Sandra. Rules have a purpose after all."

"A trial," Adrian's mother said, interrupting Sandra Huve's giggles.

"A trial? Why would I give her that?"

"You have been missing the river, haven't you Sandra? And your new shoshyuh will take some time to grow into your grandson's horse shoes."

Sandra giggled, smiling wistfully, "Yeah...Jack has been a pretty great shoshyuh, hasn't he? He deserves not to worry, right?"

"Right," Marianne cooed.

"Alright! I've made my decision. You," Sandra jabbed a long, thin finger in Sarah's direction. "You must move the flow of the great river to resume the course it ran seventy-three years ago. If you succeed, then you will be allowed to live. If not," she paused to shrug her shoulders, "then not. You understand."

Sarah did understand. She understood more when her grandmother stepped close to press a soft, velvety triangle into her hand, leaning far too close to whisper in her ear. "Thank you, for taking care of him, but your services are no longer necessary."

Adrian groaned as he came too, the wooden base of his crate unforgiving to his aching head. He shuddered and tried to shake the grogginess and ache from his body. The pain that had been bearable spiked with the motion. A coppery scent flooded the box as specks of his blood splashed the walls and floor. He swayed, falling prone as spots danced in dim light. Right. Catherine had found him.

"You need to remember what you are," she had whispered before he lost consciousness. "Meat and blood. Fuel for my house."

Adrian wasn't sure what had disturbed him more; the way she had licked and suckled her trophy, or what she did after. He could still vaguely feel her lips kissing—almost suckling—where his ear had been. Again, he shuddered, this time resisting the urge to give his body a good shake.

There was a soft noise outside of his crate; a knicker followed by a shushing told of others nearby. Aside from the wood and blood, he could smell hay and manure. Perhaps the other animals nearby could help him escape.

"Hello?" his voice was barely more than a whine. Silence fell outside, and in its presence panic began to build, squeezing his heart like an ever-tightening spring. "Please," he cried. "Please, I need help. I'm going to be killed if I'm not let out."

"You shouldn't have run from your duties," came a deep voice. "Nor should you have tried to pull others from theirs. You're a shoshyuh, yet you act like some beaten slave running from his master."

Adrian pressed his face against the inside of his box, trying to get a view of the speaker. He was too high up, the edge of a shelf blocked much of his view of the barn. "I didn't agree to die. Why do I have to lay my life down for a house that isn't even mine?"

"When you become a shoshyuh, you take on the care of all houses."

"But I never agreed to become a shoshyuh in the first place..."

Silence. Then the soft flick of horse tails and hooves scratching on the ground.

Sensing the hesitation, Adrian began with his name that of his house, and his station. Then, with still no response, he began to elaborate and explain his situation: his mother using their blood bond to force his compliance, his escape, and the naiad's instruction. Out of caution, he left mention of help from Sarah and House Thula's shoshyuh out. If he was going to die anyway, he'd rather avoid dragging others with him to Death's gate.

Silence remained his only response. The, the fluttering of feathered wings filled the space. Tiny claws scratched at the top of his box. The shimmer of gold cut off his view of the outside as those tiny claws scratched and tugged at the lock. With a click, he felt the magic of his prison recede, and his access to the Shom begin to return.

The lid opened, the familiar figure of the golden songbird illuminated in the morning light. "Sisters have mercy," she chirped. "That deranged woman harvested your ear?"

"Yeah," Adrian said as he peered over the edge of the box. There was a convenient pile of straw beneath his shelf. "Something tells me the other matrons aren't-"

The rest of his observation was lost as he and the box tumbled off the shelf. The songbird, thankfully, flew up from the box when it started to tip. Now she landed on the divider wall between the stalls.

"If you were going to say 'not like her" then you'd be correct." She twittered.

Adrian groaned, pulling himself out of the prickly straw. "I was going to say they aren't aware of what she's doing."

"They suspect it, but they aren't as crazy."

"No," Adrian shook his head and promptly regretted the motion. "Why is the Feyse matron so..."

"Blood thirsty?"

"That could be one word for it."

A deep voice, just as body-less as it had been before, supplied the answer. "Alice's curse."

"Alice?" The bird asked looking over the wall. "Wasn't she the bear shoshyuh?" Whatever motion was made on the other side seemed to answer her inquiry, as she sat back and ruffled her feathers in thought. "You have to admit that Cathy was already pretty bad before Alice took the blessing."

"Was forced," the deep voice corrected. "Just like your friend over there."

"Others have been forced into the ritual?" Adrian crawled beneath the door of his stall to look in on the speaker; four powerful golden hooves attached to muscular legs were all he could see. "I thought it was law that someone has to be willing to receive the blessing."

"The laws mean nothing to the kings and queens that wrote them," The voice continued. "Alice, visited me often while alive. I believe she would have taken the blessing on her younger sister's death had she been given time to deliver the baby. But Matron Catherine was impatient. It was likely that she hoped to obtain two shoshyuh out of the ritual with none of the other four being wise to the plan."

Adrian sat heavily on the straw, his little body not so much as disturbing the dust on the floor. Blood magic was forbidden to be used on nursing and pregnant mothers. The few that tried had died or become horribly mutated as a result. He didn't remember much of the bear shoshyuh, only knew when it had died; his grandmother had been furious upon hearing the news, as well as his mother when she had returned from performing the ritual in his grandmother's place.

Adrian cursed under his breath and staggered toward the door. The throbbing pain in his head was growing hot, uncomfortably so as his fur became caked with drying blood. He had forgotten about Sarah in his plight, but with Catherine out for blood, he didn't want to risk Sarah being left alone.

His host, however, had a different plan. The stable door creaked as it swung overhead, and the ground trembled as Adrians spotty vision became blocked by one of those four golden hooves. This one was much smaller, the gold giving way to ebony fur about half way up the leg. A midnight main braided with feathers like golden stares brushed against his face as a young horse leaned down to look at him. With a snort, her head shot back up. It was Ivy.

"There you are! What happened to your ear? Oh, Papa! This is Adrian! He's the friend I met." Her hooves pattered on the ground as she pranced in place, forcing Adrian back farther into the stall.

"Ivy." The deep voice began. "It's too dangerous for you to be here."

"I know, but-"

The songbird twittered nervously, "Honestly, Ivy this was possibly the worst time to visit your father. You have to get out of here before that crazy woman sees you."

Adrian looked up as the giddy joy started leaving those chocolate eyes of hers. "Ivy, what's going on? You're dad is the horse shoshyuh?"

The filly snorted, "Yes, silly. I'm not like you and Papa though. People want to eat me."

"Ivy here is a familiar," the songbird explained. "She inherited her Jack's intelligence and speed. Unfortunately, it is difficult to find a home for her, as she is the only one of her sisters and brothers to have the gift of speech. It would raise too many questions."

Jack, the horse shoshyuh, finally peered over his stall door, taking in Adrian and the filly with a disgruntled stare. He snorted, tossing his head as he came to a decision. "You know you weren't supposed to return here, Ivy."

Ivy stamped her foot, "I didn't plan too! I was looking for my friend."

"Then take your friend and go. Travel with him and help him finish the naiad's ritual in my place. I've no use for my blessing now anyway." As the filly's ears laid back, her large eyes filling with tears, Jack continued more gently. "I'm not mad, Ivy. Not at you. Come here. This will be my last gift for you. This time, do not return. You can't...I won't be here anymore, I won't be anywhere but in your heart. I have to fulfill my duty to House Huve."

Ivy plodded to the front of his stall door. Her muzzle was wet with the tears that ran down her nose to drip on the straw floor. She craned her neck, laying her head on the edge of the door. Jack leaned his golden head out and down, holding his daughter through the barrier. Golden energy began to swirl around them. The blessing, carried on a whispered apology, flowed from one to the other, soaking into Ivy in spreading splotches of brassy chestnut. The star between her eyes stayed golden but the rest of her coat, from nose to hoof, turned a shining brass color. Her mane and tail became like copper with strands and braids of gold. With her transformation complete, Jack stepped back to look on his daughter.

One last nod and the stallion turned to disappear into his stable. There was no goodbye, no last words. Heartbroken, Ivy cried out and pushed against the stalldoor. It didn't move. Despite his daughters cries and apologies, he did not return, nor did he say anything else. The song bird sighed, hiding her face in her front wings seeming to collect herself. Once it was clear that there would be no changing the father's mind, she flew down and began whispering to Ivy. Adrian could barely hear her soft reassurances and instead focused on staying far from the agitated hooves.

When they left, it was with a thick blanket strapped to Ivy's back. It was more comfortable than nothing but there was still no harness or bit to guide her dash from the stable. Adrian dug his claws into the fabric, praying it to be enough to hold. Stars darkened to black spots in his vision, threatening a loss of consciousness from the jostling. Faintly, he heard the songbird's cry directing them East, to the dry riverbed outside of town.

Ivy slowed, stopping on a low hill. The spots cleared from Adrian's vision, allowing him to see the dry ravine stretching before them, and the tops of houses behind. He worried that the young filly had changed her mind. He knew she had not wanted to leave, and would understand it if she chose to go back and plea to stay in the stables.

Tossing her head, the girl reared onto her back legs and belted out a cry of farewell. Filled with the fear and love of a child bound to leave a home she could never return to, it shook the threes and summoned the wind to carry it on. She set down her hooves hard, breathing heavily as she watched the stillness of the town. Her ears, pointed to the town, seemed to strain to catch any hint of a reply.

The air stilled. The distinct thrum of insects and birds resuming their afternoon discussions. Still, she waited – held by an unshakable faith in her father. The reply came in a low rumble of the ground, the wind turning to swirl around them, and the distant cry of a stallion; the cry of a father wishing his daughter a life of freedom, hope, and light.

With a final cry of remorse at their parting, Ivy turned and galloped toward the riverbed.

Adrian did his best to stay alert as they searched for Sarah along the bank. They found her a decent way from the village, a shackle on her leg chaining her to a large fallen tree. She was sitting beneath the branches when they approached, her gaze pointed toward the bank but focused on some distant thought. There was no reaction on their arrival, not until Adrian left his tentative perch on the saddle.

Sarah's bleary eyes focused on him then, "Adrian..." Tears welled in her puffy-red eyes. "I thought...I feared you were..."

"Shhh..." Adrian whispered as she bent her head to stifle her sobs. "Let's get you out of here."

"The chain," she sobbed. "They enchanted it."

They had enchanted it. Adrian read the crude inscriptions on the links, determining Sarah's punishment from the conditions. He sighed, it made sense why they would ask for the river to flow again. Riverton had once supplied the entire region with food even without the help of a shoshyuh. Since the river shifted, they barely made enough to feed themselves and make the King's tithe.

"Ivy," he asked. "I know you have your father's gift, could he do anything that could help move a river?"

Ivy shook her head. "He...Our blessing made the land fertile through the rains and storms. We also made it so others had more babies and the babies had more milk. I know how to break things though."

"Could you break this chain?"

"I can try. I haven't with metal before, but Papa could with his hooves."

Though small compared to her father, the filly still towered over Sarah and Adrian as she inspected the chain. Adrian stepped aside, wary of both hooves and flying metal. The young filly reared, her two brassy hooves glowing briefly before they crashed down on the metal with a clang. Sarah winced, covering her ears. That was when he noticed what she had been holding. It was his ear. Catherine had given her the ear for this challenge.

As Ivy reared up to hit the chain again, Adrian snatched the ear. Sarah glanced at him, not even trying to keep the scrap of flesh. She hadn't wanted it. To her it was a twisted punishment. For some reason, that small thing helped to calm his frayed nerves. Perhaps Sarah wasn't as similar to her matron as he had been fearing.

After a third attempt, the chain shattered, the enchantment releasing in a burst of energy that ruffled their hair and fur. Adrian thanked Ivy and stood over his lost ear.

With enough time, he could reattach the ear. But there was another use—one he wouldn't have considered before the previous night.

"...remember what you are. Meat and blood."

Blood was a powerful spell component. Flesh was even more powerful. When that flesh was taken from an imbued being like a shoshyuh or a familiar, miracles could be worked. With enough knowledge and skill, even mountains could be moved...or very old rivers. With the ear in his mouth he hopped down onto the river stones. He could feel the eyes of his companions on his back, but for now he ignored them.

"When you become a shoshyuh, you take on the care of all houses."

He still wasn't sure if he agreed with Jack's mentality. He hadn't agreed to this, hadn't wanted or asked for more responsibility. But there was a need.

"Ivy," he said after a moment.

"Mm-yeah?"

"Have you learned how to feel the history of a location?" He had an idea forming. Perhaps if they knew why the river stopped, then they could repair it.

"Hmm, no. I can sense there's surface water a really far way away though. Are we going to bring it here?"

"Maybe." Adrian closed his eyes. It was second nature to fell the Shom, to prepare it for his spells. This time, however, he didn't manipulate it. He watch with his heart as the threads moved with the wind and over the rocks and through the trees. It left it's mark, it always did. Sometimes that mark faded quickly, other times it left an impression—a foot print to follow.

Each stone that lines the dry riverbed had an impression. Some stones held shallow impressions, the river had been gone much longer from them, or they shifted and fell into the water long after it first flowed through the valley. Other stones, those nearest the center of the bed, held much deeper impressions. The river did not vanish all at once. Not at the start. It was lowered. The stone spoke of an old river that was miles wide that became only one mile. A sudden storm, violent and strong, and the river vanished.

With his mind, Adrian followed the stones upstream. On and on it went, around the hills cutting through trees that had long since reclaimed the edges of the bed for it's fertile soil. At it's head a mound filled the space. That mound was made of logs, debris, and other such things that had slowly strangled the stream until finally choking it out. Now the stream went a different direction. It flowed west, to city of the tree.

That complicated things.

"There's a blockage," he said with his eyes still closed. "We need to break it enough to let water through, but not all of the water. We need to split the river."

Opening his eyes, he shook the tension out of his fur and settled back into the here and now. Ivy's hooves clipped along the old stones as she joined him. Her large brown eyes held confusion as she looked from him, to the long path of stones and trees that led to the blockage. He understood her skepticism, one did not normally target something they could not see or feel. But he had seen it, and had felt it through the Shom and he had exactly what he needed to amplify his reach.

"Ivy," he said, "I need you to summon a rainstorm. I will take care of the blockage but we need the rain to help give the river a little boost."

Ivy knickered at him in relief and craned her neck down to nuzzle his furry side. Rain she could do. Raising her head to the sky, the Shom shifted around her, rustling her mane and tail with the invisible force. Adrian stepped away, not wanting to disturbe her work as he looked for an appropriate place in the river for his offering.

Finding particularly large, flat stone, Adrian placed his severed ear in the center of it. There was still plenty of shome in the flesh and fur, even without the blood. Closing his eyes once more, he focused on unraveling it. The skin, the cartilage, and every strand of fur he pulled the Shom from and directed it into the stones beneath his paws. Up the riverbed he pushed it, drawing a thin line between himself and his target. At the head of this line he gathered more Shom from the living things that had grown in place of the water. Grass whithered, flowers wilted, and seeds became innert. Even the trees, with their stocky vitality and deep roots, became ill.

The moment this tidal wave of energy reached blockage, he released the energy and broke apart the upper half of it. What little energy that remained he shaped and hardened the earth, forming a split in the river that would take many decades to become blocked again. Satisfied that the water was on its way, he released his focus. His legs trembled beneath him and his body ached. Slowly, he climbed from the stone, leaving behind the scorched symbol that had appeared in place of his ear.

A drop splashed heavily on the tip of his nose. Light, brief and wide, lit the darkened sky. Thunder followed shortly after, rumbling through as it made the smallest stones dances across the ground. Ivy released a cry far louder than he expected for a horse her size. Her spell was complete. The storm was here.

"Adrian," Sarah called. "Get out of there!"

A thin trickle of water raced between his paws. He turned to go, alarmed when the trickle grew three times in size before he reached the edge of the bank. By the time he had reached Sarah, the rain was coming down hard, and the river was a third of the way filled. The requirement of the spell had been met, and Ivy was already kneeling. Sarah laid down against the filly's back, her arms wrapped around Ivy's neck. Adrian, pinned between her and the blanket, held on for dear life.

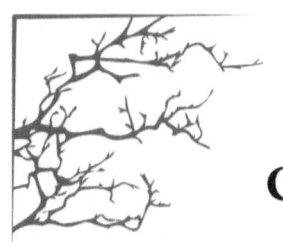

Chapter 10

The rains battered the land for hours that day. The waters of the quiet land swelled, and in a roaring rush, the river reached the Huve lands once more. Sarah, had Adrian and Ivy not come to aid her, would have been swept away in the waters. She was slated for death, either had the hands of the matrons for her failure, or by the force of the river who's return would have come with a force not even magic chains could have stopped.

That day, and that night, the three of them took shelter in the hills. Ivy's speed since her father's last gift, had become even more impressive. The dash of a few minutes took them far from the edge of the river. There, tucked into a root-filled cave, they waited. While they waited, they planned. Adrian may not have been familiar with the current relationship between the five houses, but he new the laws. Sarah, with her intimate knowledge of her own matron's fears, knew exactly which buttons to press.

It was mid-morning the following day when the storm finally abated. When they returned to the river, they saw that it had felled all but the largest trees. Branches, leaves, entire sapling lined the banks. Even as they stood there, one such sapling that had to have been at least a few years old, was caught by the current and dragged from the bank. It bobbed along, finally disappearing in the murky waters. The waters showed no sign of slowing, or of receding anytime soon. They had completed Sarah's challenge.

Now, it was time to issue their own challenge.

Sarah stepped through the gates, with her head held high. Her skirts, magically repaired, whispered against her legs as she made her way up the steps and past the guards. They didn't dare stop her, she was a house heir, and she had survived the trial. Though she stepped with confidence, inside her nerves shook from fear as much as exhaustion. Her freedom was the goal. Only her matron would know the fox had escaped again. The others, hopefully, wouldn't be interested in persuing her if she simply asked for clear passage.

Ivy had wanted her father to gain free passage too. Of course, Adrian had been against interfering with the ritual. Jack had made his choice and given what he could to aid them through Ivy. Still...it wasn't easy to loose a parent to the ritual. To know that they've been bled to the point of exhaustion, their blood staining the tables while their skin was prepared for fur.

"This is how it is, brat," her matron had said when the bowl of meat had been placed in front of her. "If you hadn't have been so useless, that would be you. Now eat it. Even if you have no magic, there are otherways you can service the Feyse."

Service. What a concept her matron pressed upon her. To bend and bleed for the house till nothing was left. The only joy in life being to see the house flourishing even as you rested on your tombstone. The thought of Ivy having to see that, having to watch her father give himself up to the houses while she watched ate away at Sarah.

But they had been too late. When Sarah had slipped into the Huve stables, Jack was gone. On his stall door, puffed up like a grim owl, was the golden bird. Those deep, beady eyes watched Sarah sneak into the dimly lit building with a distrustful glare. Sarah had stopped and the bird, sensing the girl's intent, had told her exactly what had happened with the storm broke out the previous day.

The servants opened the doors to the meeting room as Sarah continued her march into the house. The matrons sat around the oval table, their eyes glowing with the soft light of magic. Her eyes had glowed like that once. The memory twisted in her stomach like heavy stones. Even Catherine's eyes glowed, and a satisfied smile graced her ageless face.

"There's my little heir. The runner got back some time ago."

"I presume you didn't wait for that before culling Shoshyuh Jack?" The retort rolled from her tongue before she could stop herself, the venom potent enough to earn her looks from each of the matrons. Only Catherine's, to her surprise, held any malice.

"Don't start this here, brat." Catherine hiss snapped a little more sobriety into the other members.

Sandra, her eyes beginning to water with what seemed to be greif, put a hand to her mouth. Her skin lost it's color, turning a ghastly pale green. Ellen, the Willowsong matron, placed a calming hand on her sister matron's shoulder. Sandra pushed the hand away and stood up. "Don't. I know what you're going to say and you don't. None of you do."

Adrian's mother didn't seem to notice the disturbance that was right next to her. She only had eyes for Sarah. Those golden eyes held many things; grief, patience, worry, but none of it was for Sarah. Her voice was nearly cold enough to even chill Sarah's temper. "What do you want, Child?"

"Safe passage," Sarah said, allowing her head to bow to the Fultham matron. "And a single peice of the shoshyuh."

"Rather bold," Victoria of the Thula said as she reclined in her chair. "You march in and admonish us and then demand a peice of the hoard?"

Catherine snorted, "You should be grateful you survived your trial and go home."

Victoria and Ellen watched Sarah closely. Sandra's eyes flashed, looking from each of the other matrons before looking to Sarah. None of them knew why she had return. Now they wondered what her request meant. With some drunk on power and others grieving for the lost, they were too divided to make a decision quickly. Sarah only had one chance to use that division in her favor.

"What home have I?" She asked. "The only ones that truely know I'm the Feyse heir are those closest to the matrons. You have all but disowned me, having servants walk around in my place. Free Passage," she enunciated the words slowly as she sought out Sandra's watery eyes, "would at least give me dignity in my isolation."

"Dignity," the Huve matron whispered. She lowered her gaze, as if considering something. Since they were currently in her home, it was only fitting that she got the last say of any decisions. With it being her shoshyuh that had been harvested, it was respectful to consider her.

Ellen, however, had not forgotten the other part of Sarah's request. "And the piece of Jack?"

"I desire to travel a far ways." The excuse came naturally to her. "As the shoshyuh of speed and fertility, it wouldn't sit well to be without some part of him. He was dedicated to all of the houses to the very end."

"But you are leaving your house," Ellen pointed out. "What is the real reason you want it? Surely this isn't some ploy to gain an upper hand."

Sandra and Marianne's eyes widened. They gave each other a worried look. As the weakest of the five houses, any power shifts would affect them the most. Sarah hadn't thought this far. The piece wouldn't have much magic in it, not if what Adrian and Ivy said had any merit. The drunken state of the matrons wouldn't even last them the week. Already, the eyes were gaining some clarity under the pressure of decisions. She didn't even want the piece for herself.

Then she remembered the last thing he had said during their ill-fated encounter. Maybe she did want the piece for a selfish reason.

"I want it," Sarah said, "Because he was one of the last people to know my mother."

Silence followed her words. but she didn't need hear when their eyes said so much. From Catherine's accusing glare to Victoria, Marianne's confused gaze, and the quiet acceptance of Ellen. It unnerved her. Did none of them expect her to care about such a thing. Perhaps only Victoria was aware she knew. Marianne, Sarah realized with a start, wouldn't have known at all who her mother was. It would have been the previous matron of the Fulthams that attended the ceremony.

"Take it." Sandra's hoarse whisper shattered the silence.

Catherine stood, her chair falling back with a clatter. "You can't be serious in entertaining—"

"There is nothing entertaining about death, Catherine. You push and push and push for these ceremonies and completely seem to forget that the shoshyuh are our flesh and blood! Jack was my grandson. We just ate my grandson!" Sandra's fervent shouting became wailing as the horror set in.

Sarah backed away. Something was off. The high from the shoshyuh feast shouldn't have left them this quickly. Already she saw the soft glow of magic fading from them. Jack, it seemed, really had given his blessing away leaving just enough to satisfy the requirements for harvesting.

As Sandra's wailing grew louder and more distressed, the other matrons tried to console her. It was part of the sacrifice, part of the pact that kept the land stable. They couldn't break the cycle now.

But Sarah knew they could break the cycle. A few had already done so. Marianne, the second matron to have inherited her position instead of maintaining it through blood magic, met Sarah's eyes from across the room. The wailing was growing distorted, wind was picking up even though the room had no windows. "Go," Marianne mouthed as the candles began to flicker. "Save him."

And Sarah left the room. A servant, having heard the earlier command, stood outside with a lock of golden horse hair.

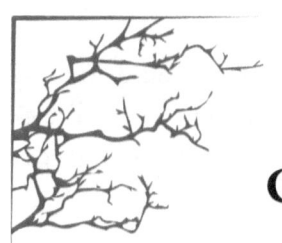

Chapter 11

Adrian listened intently as Arya informed him of what had happened inside of the room. With her small size and silent flight, the shoshyuh had easily been able to sneak into the ceremony room through the small holes at the top of the walls. He wasn't the most pleased to learn of Jack's end, or of Sarah's deviation from the plan. This time, however, the change did not result in her imprisonment.

Now he watched Sarah's approach, her leather shoes crunching on the dirt path. She had escaped, and behind her a gale wind had begun to roar around the old house. The matrons would have a hard time rebuilding if it fell. Especially without an experienced shoshyuh to guide the repairs.

"Were both of your requests granted?" Adrian asked, curious if Sarah would divulge her reasoning willingly or keep it close to her heart.

Sarah held up the lock of horsehair. She had knotted it before arriving, unwilling to lose even a single strand. The light played off of the coarse hairs, glittering as though the hair were crystalline. Though her mouth twisted in some unknown emotion, she gave the lock to Ivy.

Ivy's eyes watered, the tears overflowing to track down her cheeks and nose. "Will you braid it and hang it from my mane?"

"Of course."

"Adrian," Arya said as Sarah worked. "You should go soon. Sandra granted the girl's pardon, but Catherine may still seek you out. The next location is your house. You need to find your sister before we meet again at the tree."

"You will be able to join us?"

"I will at the right time. I am not restrained in the same way that the other Shoshyuh are. I must lay eggs and rear young enough to sate Victoria's need for magic. I will meet you there, do not fear about that. In the mean time," Arya trailed off to pluck at her plumage. A feather, perhaps no longer than Adrian's nose, came free, "Have Sarah fix that into your fur. It is not much, but it may help protect you if the shadow hounds find you."

Adrian shuddered. He did not want to see the red eyes and sharp teeth again. They needed to leave before Sandra's outburst was calmed. The wind and storm from her distress still raged on, but in the shadows of the mansion, lights began to move. They moved in crimson pairs, searching the grounds for that which had escaped their master. Adrian's ears dropped. Lily had no idea what had happened to him after his escape and he had no idea of what had happened to her. Their mother and the other matrons would not have taken kindly to his stunt at the banquet and Lily could have taken the fall.

His grandmother's words trailed back into his mind. His sister was in just as much danger as any of the shoshyuh. Suddenly, his hesitation was gone, completely replaced by the urge to see her safe and sound.

"We need to go." Adrian leapt onto Ivy's back. "Back toward the barrows, but farther."

Sarah had just finished the last knot and had reached for Arya's feather when she also saw them. Wordlessly, she hopped onto the mare's back. With a deft movement of her fingers, she secured the feather on his shoulder enough for Arya to magically finish the knot.

There was no time for goodbyes as they plunged into the forest. There was no time for planning as they became a blur in the wind. The hounds had seen them and followed even as Arya returned to safety.

Ivy's speed and grace, enhanced by her father's blessing, was the only reason they were not overtaken immediately. But each second brought the hounds ever closer until they were nipping at the mare's hooves and tail. The farther they got from the House of Huve, however, the less speed the hounds had until they were just barely keeping up. However, Adrian knew that just one wrong move, one stumble or a log that made them slow a little too much on landing, and the wolves would have them.

"Adrian," Ivy called. Fatigue ate at her voice, breathless from the dash across the land. Immediately he saw her concern, in the glimpse of a roaring river. It was the river they had just moved. Flooded and filled from the storm, it churned and cut through the land on it's ancestral path to the sea. The hounds were going to drive them right into the murky rapids.

They came nearer, precious seconds ticking by. Adrian's brain froze, the hounds were too close. If they turned or stopped, they would be caught. If they plunged into the cold waters they might not survive. He looked around, desperate for a different way, a different path they could take.

"Jump the river," Sarah called over him.

"It's too big," Ivy cried. "I'll fall and drown."

"It's not too big. Remember your papa, he could jump rivers no problem."

"But I'm too small, Papa was huge compared to me!"

"But you have in your mane a feather from Arya! It will give you the extra boost you need."

Ivy squealed as a hound bit her flank. Blood, dark and thick, flecked her brassy fur and she swerved, smashing the creature between her flank and a tree. She was free, but only for a second. The sound of their pursuit was still too close and steadily fading under the sound of the river's flow.

It was too late now. They needed to jump or give up.

Ivy jumped.

Adrian closed his eyes tight as Ivy's hooves flashed and the feather in her main flashed with light. Then they were in the air, weightless except for the stones in their stomachs with rolled and clattered around. The water below opened it's maw, as if to receive them, and then closed it again. With a splash, they landed near the opposite edge. They made it, but they weren't free.

With Sarah's urging, Ivy pulled herself free of the mud and continued their flight through the woods. The hounds, unable to cross the flowing stream, were left behind. Unable to return without the shoshyuh, they melted into the shadows. Adrian felt those red eyes follow them, burning his skin and fur with hatred before they were finally out of sight.

They had made it. But the freedom was not without cost. On reaching the barrows they stopped. Ivy's wound had swollen, the fur taking a rusted tone as the skin beneath it reddened. Adrian shuddered and looked at Sarah with a helpless look in his eyes. Never had he seen a wound fester so rapidly. Sarah, on the otherhand, seemed bleak as she stared at the wound.

"It hurts," Ivy whined, stopping the leg as if that would rid her of the wound.

"It's a cursed wound," Sarah said calmly. "My m...Catherine uses the hexes with her hounds when she hunts runaway servants. Only powerful healing magic will remove the pestilence."

Adrian's ears laid back as Sarah's eyes turned toward him. He knew how to repair curtains and glass. Living beings and disease were an entirely different matter. But it wasn't his magic that Sarah had in mind.

"We need your sister." Her arms scooped up Adrian and placed him back on the saddle. Soon her weight was settled behind him. "Ivy, we need to get to the edge of the Fultham property. Adrian, how do I get to your sister without alerting the servants."

Adrian blinked, his mind taking precious seconds to catch up to the current situation. "Ah, you would have to find her when she's in the bath. That's the only time she's not coddled up in the attic or surrounded by servants. You do understand that if you are seen close to her the guards could kill you on site instead of waiting for my mother to return for your trial, right?"

"Surely your sister wouldn't-"

"My sister is mute."

Ivy limped along as silence fell between the two of them. Despite her slow gait, Adrian noticed the trees were still passing them at a considerable speed. Once, he had been told that all shoshyuh paid a price for their blessing. Now he wasn't so sure. Of all the shoshyuh, Lily was the only one incapable of speech. He wished he could remember if her predecessor was also mute, but he had been so young when she vanished. If Lily had been made mute, perhaps it could be reversed. If not, then maybe he could help her find her voice the way he had found his own.

They were nearly to the parameter of the house when Ivy collapsed beneath an old tree. The house was in site, far from the village lines unlike the houses of other matrons they were both exposed and hidden. Adrian hopped carefully from the saddle to look again at the wound. The swelling had spread, and the flesh had grown hot. Again, Ivy cried about the pain. He wanted to go fetch his sister himself, but he couldn't leave Ivy like this. With a sigh he began gathering threads of Shom. There was one way he could help, it wouldn't buy them any time, but it would ease his friend's suffering.

"Sarah," he said as he carefully focused on the gathering energy, "Go get my sister. Go under the cover of night and wait for her to be left alone in the bath house. Go to her and explain briefly that you are a friend and Adrian sent you to rescue her. Do not allow her to say goodbye to anyone...even if she cries."

Sarah straightened, her concern for Ivy fading behind a wall of determination, "I'll get it done."

"Go. Bring her back safely."

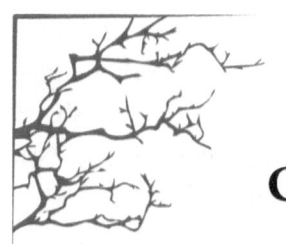

Chapter 12

S arah left before Ivy had fully succumbed to Adrian's magic. Since it was still light out, she took cover in the gardens. At least here she was in her element. He was just a girl to be ignored by servants and house members alike. She inspected the rose hips, admired the peaches that were late to ripen, whatever took the attention off herself. Guards were more alert near the house, their eyes clear of the groggy fog that plagued the grounds keepers. It made sense, keep the more focused guards closer to the more valuable items.

The bath house, unfortunately, was near the house. Sarah had to fight the urge to sneak in before the servants had prepared it. She didn't know what the inside looked like, and if she was seen lurking, they may raise an alarm and keep the shoshyuh locked inside the house. She looked at the house, tempted to climb the winding ivy and morning glory vines instead. But she didn't know if Lily would be able to climb down unassisted, or if they would be more easily be seen.

Adrian was busy with Ivy, of course she'd be seen. Sarah sighed, as she inspected the petals of a rather large violet. Without Adrian's help, she wasn't sure how she would accomplish the task. She hadn't even been able to accomplish such a feat with his help.

But then...she had made a mess of those herself, hadn't she?

Her jaw tensed, agitation building as she went back over the events. She had been the one to try and take the golden acorns. Again, she had been the one to try and force a shoshyuh to leave with her. She couldn't risk finding a new mistake. Not with Ivy and Adrian depending on her getting this right.

When night finally came, Sarah found a small alcove near the stables to hide in. The bathhouse was in site. Servants rushed back and forth with buckets of water and a small hearth fire crackled inside, it's flames causing flickering shadows to dance across the yard. The bath didn't seem to be that large since not many buckets were brought inside before a small group approached the structure. Two guards. Three servants. It seemed a woefully small number after the trouble Sarah had caused at the other houses; but perhaps it wasn't known that trouble had been caused at all. It was a theory she could use to her advantage.

Adrian's warning echoed in her head, shaking lose the thought of approaching directly. She had to wait, even though her hands wrung and fidgeted with impatient energy. The guards stayed outside, their backs turned to the door. That was fine. There was a window at the back of the structure. Was was not as fine was that the figure that vanished with the servants was well covered. Sarah had no way to know for sure that that was the shoshyuh, or an important guest.

No. She had to have a little faith.

Soon, the servants had finished bathing Lily and allowed her some privacy. They filtered out, on at a time to chat with the guards while they waited for some signal that their charge was ready to return to her room. Sarah let them be, slipping from shadow to shadow until she found the window at the back of the small building. The shutters were open, likely to allow in the cool night breeze.

Lily was sitting in the wooden tub, her nack to the window as Sarah crept in. Her shoulders were shaking despite the steam that rose from the bath. Her golden hair, having already been washed and combed, was piled on top of her head, pinned in place by thin copper sticks. Sarah edged forward, slowly coming around to kneel at the side of the tub. Lily, didn't look at her, she didnt seem to be looking anywhere.

Her emerald eyes were glassy, the flesh around them pink and swollen from tears. Sarah reached out, slow so at to not startled her, her hand trailing closer and closer until it felt the warm, smooth skin of Lily's shoulder. The eyes snapped to attention and focused on Sarah. Surprise flashed there, without anger or fear.

But she didn't pull away.

Sarah blushed, her face growing hot as she took in the maiden's appearance. She was a tall girl, the water only barely reached the bottom of her comely breasts. She wasn't a thin girl by any means. She was shapely, with a oval face and large emerald eyes. In those eyes, Sarah could see a flash of gold just as her hand warmed from the brief exchange of magic between them. The maiden was scared, but not of her. She seemed scared of what could have arrived instead of her.

Water dripped from Lily's pale arm as she reached up to touch Sarah's cheek. Sarah let her, there wasn't a reason to avoid the touch even though it left a line of water to drip down her jaw.

"Come with me," Sarah whispered softly. "Your brother waits for you with a friend."

Lily pulled back. Wariness flashed in her eyes as they flicked toward the door.

"You can't. You know they won't let you go."

Again those eyes met hers, the emerald seas pleading. There was someone else she loved here, someone she worried for.

"Your mother?"

A slow nod.

"Lily," Sarah hesitated. She would have wanted the same, had her father been alive. She too looked toward the door. There wouldn't be another chance. Not when they figured out there had been a visitor. "I'm sorry. Your brother and our freind need you. Now is the best time, while your mother is still at House Huve."

The eyes widened, those pale lips parted in a silent 'Oh'.

"She didn't tell you she was gone?"

A slow shake of her head. A strand of golden hair was sliding loose, threatening to fall back into the warm water. Sarah wasn't thinking as she reched out to tuck the strand back into the mane of hair. The feelings she had, was this an affect of the magic that passed between them? She would have to ask Adrian later. For now, she enjoyed the brief moment of content quiet as Lily thought over her words.

A shuffle outside. Impatient guards whispered to the serving women. The emerald seas widened again, and searched the room for something, somewhere to hide. One of the voices grew louder, they wanted to check on her. Those wet, warm hands suddenly grabbed Sarah's dress top, pulling her down. There was barely a moment to take a breath before the world became flooded. Another world, dark except for the glitter of candlelight on the fractured ceiling opened before her. He hadn't thought such magic was possible. Beneath the maiden, a ledge had formed that led into water deep enough to hide both Sarah and her clothes.

The dull thump of the door was hard to hear in the small pocket of warped reality. Hands, gentle but firm despite their trembling, held her well below the surface of the water. Sarah remained still, the burning need for air started deep in her throat as muffled voices sounded overhead. They asked about a visitor, whatever answer Lily gave seemed to satisfy them. They expected a visitor to see Lily soon. Sarah's mind churned as the burn spread deeper into her lungs. She needed air. She also needed to not be caught.

There was a dull thump, the light flickered but stayed lit. The hands changed their grip and pulled instead of pushed. Sarah struggled to stay quiet as she broke the surface. She coughed, as quietly as she could manage into her hands. "Who..."

Lily placed a finger on Sarah's lips. Her face was pale. Emerald seas shimmered with the threat of rain as they sought the back window. Sarah nodded, seeing that Lily was ready to go. Whomever the servants expected Lily to meet, the woman clearly did not want to meet. Sarah rose, her dress clinging to her skin uncomfortably as it dripped back into the bath water. Sarah froze, glancing to the door. The servants continued their idle chatter with the guards.

Lily tugged at the dress, pushing Sarah back under the water to peel the fabric from her. Sarah twisted, helping Lily undress her. Finally the dress and it's layers floated about them. Sarah shivered, the wind raising bumps over her exposed shoulders and chest. Lily rose slowly, guiding Sarah by the hand to do the same. Finally they stood and as one stepped from the basin. Through it all the servants didn't cease chattering.

There was only one dress an accompanying layer. The fabric was soft, but clung too easily to damp skin as Sarah picked it up. Lily was already trying to slip out of the open window. Throwing the dress over her shoulder, Sarah followed the shoshyuh. How they were not seen, even by the guards or the servants, did not sit well with her. Someone should have looked. Someone should have been watching each side of the building.

As they neared the edge of the property, Lily slowed. She looked back, the moonlight outlining each jagged edge of her home. Sarah hadn't looked back when she had left. There hadn't been a reason to. But Lily's childhood wasn't hers. Sarah hadn't been attached to anyone, hadn't felt wanted by anyone. The trembling of Lily's hands made them feel so fragile as Sarah guided her away—yet also the same. It was a little warmer. A little paler. It was flesh and blood. It was human.

They were human.

Her father had been human.

Bile rose in Sarah's throat as they fled. The prick of grass on her bare feet, the scratch of branches and dried leaves against her chilled legs, and the warmth of Lily's hand kept her from slipping. It kept the memory at bay, but it lingered there at the edge of her mind. Each step she began to feel as though it were that memory, that night in her life, that she was fleeing from. That she was trying to take Lily from. She pushed them to move a little faster, the small stones and pebbles sending sharp pinpoints of pain through her feet.

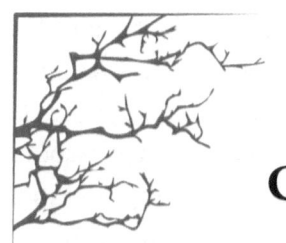

Chapter 13

Ivy's pulse weakened as the moon crept closer to its zenith. Adrian bowed his head and brushed a lock of the mare's mane back with his nose. Her fur was wet, salty with sweat as she flinched in her sleep. Through the Shom, he held her close just between dreaming and waking. It was necessary to keep the nightmares away. At least here, in the nebulous void, her body could focus on fighting the curse, and her mind would not remember the battle.

He felt the souls approaching before he heard the crunch of their feet on the dried leaves. He turned only to avert his eyes. Naked. Both of the women were naked, their breath puffing from their mad dash. His fur rose between his shoulder blades, his tentative hold over Ivy slipping from the distraction.

Then he was pulled against his sister's chest. Her energy bled into his, their Shom raveling together like sturdy thread. Ivy fell back into her dreamless sleep and the curse began to abate. Lily's magic expanded, filling him, soothing the pain from his wounds, then spilling over into Ivy. The mare relaxed, the swelling receded, and the wound began to shrink. She was healing both of them, even though it was exhausting herself in the process.

"Lily, it's okay."

She shook her head, holding him tighter. The back of his neck, where she hid her face, he began to feel the fur damped by her tears. A choked sob was her reply...and she was right. It wasn't okay. None of this was okay. They needed to move soon. Ivy wouldn't have much time to heal with sunrise approaching.

His ear twitched as the house bells broke the stillness of the night. "Lily, we need to go."

Her hold on him tightened, uncomfortable but he bore it quietly. He could feel her power calming, helping him to wake Ivy. The curse was gone. But the wound remained.

The mare shot to her feet, panting and backing away. Then, as if realizing it was not foes before her, her breathing slowed. The horns were still sounding. In the courtyards, specks moved about. Horses, guards, servants, they were gathering for the search.

"Can you carry riders?" Adrian asked.

Ivy inspected the injury and took a few tentative steps. The leg held...barely.

Sarah shook her head. "We shouldn't risk it."

Lily said nothing, accepting the clothes around Sarah's neck and putting them on. There was open field between them and the forming search party, but to their west there was a stand of trees. It had been used for hunting in his grandmother's time, but now it had grown wild. Calling the others to hurry, he led them toward it's cover.

"Stay together," he called. "Sarah, Lily, stand beside Ivy, keep her between you and the house so they don't see you."

They moved together slowly with Adrian in the lead. The grass was just tall enough for him to crouch down in, and with the heavy rain his light steps did not make much sound.

He wished it were the same for their steps. The ground was soft. Puddles of mud barred them from making a straight path toward the trees. The search party was far behind, still trying to pick up the trail the two girls had left in the night. They were not far enough away, however, for Adrian to miss the baying of dogs.

The idiots, Adrian thought viciously, using dogs to track a shoshyuh was asking for the shoshyuh to be injured on the way back. He had to think fast. The forest, though dense, was not far enough away to give them a strong head start. With Ivy still trying to recover, there wasn't an easy way out of the predicament. As he was looking around, hoping for some clue or animal den they could use to distract the dogs, he neglected to look ahead of himself and stepped right into a shallow puddle.

The water rippled, the mud swirling up after his paw before beginning to settle back down. It fell slowly, spreading more than falling. The result was a very murky puddle which he could not see the bottom of. With the surface of the water still once more, he could barely make himself out through the murk. It was as if he were a shade, looking out at a more colorful and vibrant world.

Adrian turned to face the group, "I have an idea. Do you think you can summon more rain Ivy? I don't need a lot, just a drizzle."

"I think so, does this mean we can rest a little?"

"Only for a little while," he cautioned. With the feast of Jack having already concluded, time was quickly diminishing before the matrons were on the move again—if they hadn't already begun the hunt.

"Is there anything we can do?" Sarah stepped forward, Lily close to her side.

Adrian closed his eyes for a moment to gather his wits. How Sarah managed to lose her dress, he might never understand. When he opened his eyes again his sister was signing something. She had caught on to his plan, and had an idea of her own. Something to spook the guards away for a day or two and direct them elsewhere. His jaw slackened as he carefully read each sign, then his blood began to burn with rage. Now he understood one of his mother's strange answers, and made his fur stand on end.

They took their positions, hidden carefully in the bushes and trees of the small stand. Adrian watched from the relative dryness of a burrow, cradled by tree roots. Nearby, Ivy nickered softly, the air shimmering with the magic of her call. The sky, which had already been overcast, darkened overhead. The muted clip of horse hooves on the soft ground followed the whine of the hunting dogs. Animals were always sensitive to magic, they could feel it just like they could the wind. Just this once, it didn't make much difference if the dogs found the bait, or bolted.

Commands barked from their masters. The whining grew both nearer and quieter. As the first horse to step into the forest gave a firm stamp of protest, Adrian released a long, high-pitched warble. The magic he had wove into the misting rain released on his call. A shade, a pale girl with long golden hair tore through the bushes. The hunt was on. Between and around the trees the girl flew; leaves and branches sheltered her even as they cut into her pursuers. At times she vanished only to appear again farther away.

When finally she allowed them to draw near, she stood atop a rock with a crude rope in her hand. They called off the dogs as the girl sliped the rope around her neck. A servant stepped forward to plea with her. She needed to think of her mother and of her brother serving the Feyse; and when she stepped back a slender foot dangling off the edge of the rock, she needed to think of her house and her duty to them to bare an heir. At that, the girl smiled, and slipped from the edge. The fall was short and the rope weak, but it was strong enough. The servants flew forward, slicing the rope and holding the still body close.

It didn't matter. There was no pulse.

Adrian's stomach twisted as the servants began their wail. He suspected his sister was right, but it didn't sit well with him. He knew she was safe with Ivy, hidden away from where they had planted the doll. But as the party picked up the pale form, he could see the bruising the rope had left around its neck. It had been a doll. A creation that combined his and Lily's magic with locks of his sister's hair, it was a near-perfect replica. The only difference was that it's heart had never beat.

When it became clear that the hunting party had accepted it's role as a mourning party, he slipped away. The brief moment he had seen the doll hanging there, swaying ever so slightly in the wind, gave him an acrid taste. He needed to drive the image from his mind, and they needed to get away from the Fultham territory.

Lily, well aside from the shadows of fatigue that framed her eyes, was crouched behind Ivy. Sarah's arms were around her, almost as if to sheild his sister from the world. Adrian would have found the sight endearing had they been hiding under different circumstances. He emerged from the bushes, signaling Ivy. All three of the women rose and without a word, followed him out of the stands and back around toward the barrows. There wouldn't be much in the barrows, but there would be clothes, and there would be shelter for a short time.

"How long do you think we have?" Sarah asked. Though the walk had been long, the decoy had worked to prevent any other hunting parties from tailing them. Now they huddled around a small fire Adrian had conjured, deep within one of the older burrows.

"A few days at most," he answered. His stomach growled, complaining at the lack of food that the grave had to offer. He ignored it for now. Sleep seemed more pressing.

'Where will we go?' Lily signed to him.

Having given her clothes and hair to the dummy, she looked far removed from the noblewoman she was. At least Sarah had been able to shape her hair with the front just a few inches shy of her shoulders, though the back was still to short for her liking. Adrian could tell by the why she would reach behind her to pull the hair forward, only to stop and drop her hand back into her lap. Her and Sarah had managed to find clothes among the offerings left behind with the dead. With the image of her doll still swaying beneath the forst canopy, it unsettled him to see her in the plain white and blue burial dress. At least, he reassured himself, neither of the women had needed to take clothes directly from a slumbering corpse.

"To the shoshyuh tree. The bird will meet us there so we can hopefully break the curses us."

'The blessing is powerful magic, reversing it has never been done.'

"I don't care about becoming human anymore."

That seemed to make her pause. Her brows knit together, and she suddenly seemed less certain of the situation. To Adrian, a little bit of uncertanty wasn't a bad thing. It made them wary, which would hopefully keep them alive long enough for the ritual. He sat up and, meeting her gaze, began to explain what had happened since he had escaped the banquet. The journal, the ghosts, even the mishaps in trying to speak to the other shoshyuh. The nymph, he waited until the end to tell her about. While not the first or the last, the words of the nature spirit were the closest to an answer he had gotten.

"Her instructions were to remove my paws and head. Between that and what I've learned from the others, I need all of us to perform the ritual." Lily had begun to shake her head, her eyes hardening with denial. "Please, it's the only way to free us."

Lily brought her hand across the air in a clear demand. She didn't want to hear it. It didn't matter if he was a fox or some other form. She was not going to help in the ritual. She was not going to help him die.

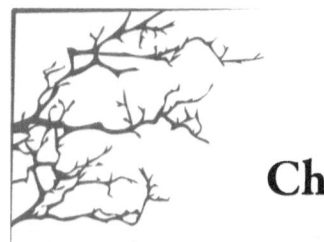

Chapter 14

"What do you mean you're not going to help?"

Sarah tensed. The air between the siblings was charged, their anger and shock almost palpable. No words or motions passed between them, but they came to some understanding. Lily shot to her feet and marched deeper into the barrow. Adrian bit back a growl, the sound cutting off as he turned away.

Sarah and Ivy shared a look. This spell was not going to be powerful enough without all five of the shoshyuh helping. Iv, having been gifted the power, was the only one of them that had no bindings on her. She could leave, but the others could not. Even Sarah, with her magic locked away, didn't have much hope of being free of her matron. The woman seemed to know where she was at all times.

The uncomfortable silence continued through the night. Sarah took the first watch, listening to the twins shuffle around as sleep eluded them. In the light of dawn, tear streaks glittered on Lily's cheeks. Adrian again approached her, his ears and tail down cast as he tried his plea a second time. Lily turned away, unwilling to hear him out.

It was the second day of this silence when Ivy was well enough to travel. The siblings silently used what power they had regained to finish healing the mare as they left. Lily's funeral would happen any day now. They couldn't risk Catherine getting too close again, a run-in with her shadow hounds would mean death for them.

So they rode in silence. Sarah's arms were wrapped tight around Lily's waist as they rode together. Adrian balanced as well as he could behind her, while Lily held on tight to Ivy's mane. Trusting Ivy to get them to the Oak City in one peice, Sarah laid her head against Lily's shoulder. The woman was tense, fear and sadness seemed to roll from her in waves. It took her mind back to the banquet where she looked so regal, and then to the bath where she seemed so defenceless.

"I know it scares you," Sarah whispered. "The chance of losing him."

Silence, and then a sniffle. She shook her head. It wasn't just a chance to her.

The Maiden had once been referred to as the Seer before the lineages became so focused on the maternal line. Sarah hid her face against the fabric of Lily's dress. "You've seen the outcome?"

A subtle nod. Of course, she had seen it. She had known since Adrian had been selected that death waited for him. As his sister, she wouldn't have left any path unexplored that her powers could reach.

For Sarah, the news was more troubling. She had wanted to prevent the slaughter of more shoshyuh, yet here she was helping one to his death. But then, without the magic they would stay trapped, forever bound by their house to obey. In the end, all she could do was watch, and help the shoshyuh manage their own choices—even if they didn't agree with each other.

"Lily, he's..."

A gentle hand, warm from Ivy's mane, slid over her own. Lily's fingers laced with hers, squeezing tight. She knew, Sarah realized. And so she returned the squeeze and held Lily tighter as they both shed silent tears. At her back, Adrian curled up, pressing against her. Whether he was trying to stay on Ivy, or if he was trying to comfort them, Sarah wasn't sure.

Arya met them a mile away from the city edge. The bird glimmered like a second sun in the light of day. Ivy stopped beneath the tree she landed on, panting slightly from her exertion.

"You got away," Sarah said.

"I was let out," Arya corrected. "If you think Victoria has been kept completely ignorant of this situation then you are sadly mistaken. She likes the power gained from the shoshyuh, but Catherine's instability is a much larger threat."

Adrian bounded around Sarah and his sister to stand on the back of Ivy's head. "So she's letting you help us?"

"Yes, just like Ellen is going to help you as well."

"But she's a matron," Sarah added. "What if the ritual changes the oak shoshyuh into a person again?"

"Then Ellen and Nicolas will finally be reunited."

Sarah and Adrian exchanged a glance. There was so much more to the history than either of them knew.

Ivy craned her neck upward, blinking adoringly at the bird. "Is the tree's name Nicolas?"

"Yes, dear. But that's enough questions for now. I came to tell you to go to the southern gate. One of Ellen's servants has been instructed to let you onto the grounds. She will not be able to join you for another day or two and asks that you wait for the daughters at House Willowsong."

"But the longer we wait, the closer Catherine gets to us." Sarah said.

"Catherine would have to know where you are, to get close to you. Your meeting with her at House Huve was an unfortunate coincidence. Not only that, but you have Ivy with you. Escape is a small feets as long as you are with her."

"But Arya," Ivy whined. "I can't outrun the shadow hounds. See?" Turning she showed her hip to the bird. Though Adrian and Lily had done what they could, a jagged crescent scar had remained.

Arya surveyed the injury with a grim acceptance in her beady eyes. "Perhaps not by yourself. But as long as you have another shoshyuh with you, you should be able to outrun even those creatures. Come, meet me beneath the tree and I will tell you what I know."

Before any more questions or objections could be raised, Arya left her perch. Sarah watched her go, the flickering glimmer of her wings dazzling in the afternoon sunlight. Ivy sighed and began plodding toward the southern entrance to the city. Adrian slid down the mare's neck, resting against his sister as he watched the road ahead with a faraway look.

Sarah's attention stayed on the road. With them moving at a speed unaided by magic, the trees and bushes slid past them at a reasonable pace. The road was well-packed, sand and stone had been used to furrows dug by wagons loaded with crops. The trees gave way to flat farmland. The workers were out, tending to the season's last harvest in the afternoon heat. Farmers that looked up marveled at the odd group. A glimmering brass horse trotting along with an unnaturally blonde fox and two strangely dressed women on its back was likely the most interesting sight the farmers would see for years.

Sarah focused on the road ahead. Perhaps she should have asked Adrian to check his grandmother's barrow for more modern clothes. As it was, the long gowns with the split skirts and trousers were a stark contrast against the plain dresses of the farm wives and young women. Their hair was loose, instead of bound up and hidden beneath cowls. Lily's hair was too short to put into plates. It was a small relief when parents and other adults prevented the children from running up to them. Fewer questions meant more speculation. Speculation led to tales that weren't believable.

The gate rose before them; the iron was rusted by years of wind and rain, the wood had not fared much better as gray fungi jutted out from the frame in shelf-like form. The guards gave them a simple nod and allowed them to pass without question. Sarah's lips drew in to a tight line. It was too easy, she thought, after all the running and the threats, this matron was welcoming them in. Of the three shoshyuh with her, only Adrian seemed tense as he perched on Ivy's back. The fox had stretched himself out, planting his front paws firmly against the back of Ivy's neck. His ears and nose twitched as he took in the wood and daub buildings of the small city.

Sarah's unease lessened only a fraction when they were allowed to travel directly into the courtyard of House Willowsong. With trumpet vines and dark leafy creepers clinging to it's walls, the damage of age was well hidden. As Ivy brought them nearer, however, Sarah could make out cracks in the stone base, and more strange fungus growing in the partially rotted wood. There was no glass, but the shutters and latches appeared new—the wood shined with oil.

A house servant led them around the side where a small stable stood. The roof sagged beneath the weight of the crawling vines, and the stalls inside were empty save for one old mare. Ivy threw her head back, nearly tossing Adrian as she shook out her mane.

"I don't think she wants to be in the stall," Sarah said to the servant. "Could she come with us to the tree?"

"A horse...visiting the Great Tree?" The servant's eyebrows nearly disappeared into her headscarf.

Sarah glanced at Adrian, but the fox stared passively at the stable, feigning the role of a tamed pet. Sarah pulled her shoulders back, giving the servant a bored look. "I will rephrase. My mare is not trained for stables and I would like to keep her close. Is there room for her to graze beneath the Great Oak or is there a pasture she can roam while staying within sight of the house?"

The woman paled and clasped her hand together in front of her skirts. "I cannot give your mare access to the Great Tree, but I can open the pasture for you." Turning, she led them behind the stable where old wooden gates led the way into an open pasture. There were a few goats, but otherwise it was empty.

Sarah could only sigh in response. Adrian hadn't said anything as if he were just Lily's strange colored pet. What she could and couldn't say, she had no guidance on, erring on the side of caution seemed the best route.

They dismounted Ivy together, and the mare tread into the pasture. It took only a moment for her to see something glimmer in the distance, and then race after it across the field. Sarah breathed a relaxed sigh. It would not have surprised her if Ivy refused to enter the fenced area. The mare was a free spirit. However it seemed the golden bird had made good on her word to meet them as the little songbird flew down to land on the blankets that were still strapped to the mare's back.

Satisfied that Ivy was well taken care of, Sarah allowed the serving woman to lead them inside. On passing the threshold, Sarah and Lily shared a wide-eyed look. Adrian sat up in Lily's arms looking around with his nose twitching at the smells that were coming through the halls. Sarah took a deep breath in. Wildflowers and honey hung in the air. The floors shone with a wax. Walls held tapestries of deep and rich colors and little fraying.

Cracks could still be seen peaking between decorations as they snaked up the walls, but they were covered in a paste-like mixture of tar and sap. There was no glass to be seen in the windows, but it wasn't needed. On the inside of the shutters were illustrations of distant lands, castle chambers, and caves decorated with various crystals. The servant must have expected such surprise from the guests as she stopped to allow them to admire the art that surrounded them.

"This was the original home of Princess Ellenora, the youngest of the sisters." The servant smiled as she gestured to one tapestry of a castle framed by tall aspen trees. "This is an original depiction of the castle which the royal blood was born and prospered in until the Red War. If you look closely, you can find each of the sisters and their symbols in the image."

"Thank you, Amberline," a calm voice said from farther down the hallway. "That will be all."

With a bow, the servant departed. Their new host was young man with golden eyes and hair. Even dressed in a simple cotton tunic and dark trousers, the stranger held himself with an assured confidence that couldn't be attributed to a normal house servant. Sarah said nothing. Lily's hand found hers, squeezing tightly as she too, realized it wasn't an ordinary human to stand before them. He was another shoshyuh, one like Lily that had retained a human form.

"I'm Alexandra," he said, lowering his eyes briefly. "Third shoshyuh of the Five Houses."

"What...?" Adrian jumped from Lily's arms to pad closer to the man. "But Lily is our shoshyuh...My grandmother said the rest had died."

"A slight exaggeration," their host replied softly as he sat on his knees before the fox. "Very few are willing to eat the heart of their children. My mother hid me away under the boughs of the Great Oak."

Lily's hand tightened around Sarah's, almost painful as the woman stared at Alexandra.

"You have a voice," Sarah said. "You weren't silenced by the shoshyuh ritual?"

Alexandra shook his head, "The curses were added to the ritual well after me."

"So we really are cursed?" Adrian asked. "All of us that came from this generation of shoshyuh?"

Alexandra rose and, motioning for them to follow, led them through the house as he spoke. "Most of you, yes. After the power of the shoshyuh was realized, the five decided that it would be best to place some sort of shackle on them. These took the form of blood bindings, animal forms, loss of speech...the list became endless until each house decided what they could and could not do without in regards to a shoshyuh. The four that dedicated themselves to use of shoshyuh for harvesting decided on the blood bindings and one reduction of ability. For three, this was a conversion from the human to the animal. For one, it was the loss of voice."

Beyond the halls of the house, doors opened to a center courtyard. The grass was thick with wildflowers, with bushes thick with leaves and berries. The area was blanketed in a dappled shade, above them only pinpoint of sky could be seen through the thick golden leaves of the Great Oak. Alexandra stepped out onto the grass, his bare feet sinking among the soft blades as he motioned for them to join him.

"This," he said as he sat down with his back against the tree, "Is Nicolas, Shoshyuh of the Five Sisters, and Great Tree of House Willowsong. He will be leading tonight's ritual."

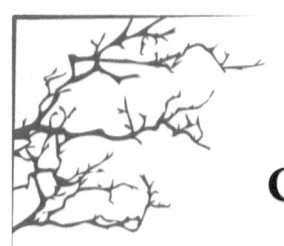

Chapter 15

"Tonight?" Anxiety shot through Sarah's chest as true as any arrow. She wasn't ready, Lily still hadn't agreed, and they hadn't figured out how to get Ivy into the tree's garden. "Weren't we going to wait for Matron Willowsong?"

"My mother will not make it in time," Alexandra reassured her. "Nicolas and I believe that to wait would be too dangerous. Catherine is on her way and mother is currently attempting to mislead her."

"Already?" Adrian said, "But we rode Ivy."

"The magical speed of the young shoshyuh does little to hide her from the nose of a wolf. The ritual will need to happen tonight, or the curse over the shoshyuh will not be broken and many of you will die."

Silence followed. Sarah had thought only Adrian was in threat of dying, but then she hadn't known about Catherine's hunger. She felt the tremble start in her arms as the memory of her father's meat rose unbidden and unwanted. Lily's weight against her side, warm and real. A glow, soft and silver, appeared in the corner of her vision. It was Lily. The gold in her eyes was split by a silver ring.

She had never felt the Shom until that moment. It was like a fog that had settled around them, cool and heavy. It shifted and swirled around on invisible winds, never fully settling, never going beyond the surface of her skin. But when she looked at Lily, the Shom moved through her. It was a part of her. It painted images around her that her eyes read like the pages of a codex. Adrian climbed onto his twin's lap, the Shom soaking into his fur as he moved. Then his eyes glowed as well, and he too read the images in the Shom.

Sarah stared at the Shom in wonder. This is what she had never seen, never felt, before now. It was like a piece of a puzzle, stolen away before she could ever know it was there. Alexandra was staring at her with a mixture of awe and understanding. Confused, she looked down. She was still human. Her clothes were still those from the barrows, but it was a lock of glittering brass hair fell across her face instead of brown. She pulled her hair in front of her shoulders to see that it was streaked with brassy locks. Again, she met those deep golden eyes of the ancient shoshyuh. The nymph was right. She had magic...it was just locked away. She was cursed like the others.

Like a shift in the wind, the Shom swirled around them and vanished. Sarah's hair returned to it's normal brown tones. Tears where trailing down the cheeks of both twins. Lily let go and gathered Adrian up into her arms to hold him as they cried together. She looked away, her stomach twisting into knots. Alexandra rose, and with a polite bow, left to gather the items for the ritual.

In the distance, a wavering howl rose. Catherine had summoned her shadow hounds. It was time. The ritual had to happen now or never.

Alexandra returned without a sound, his eyes glowing as he called on the Shom to guide him. Ivy was led in, Arya riding on the mare's back through the mansion. Sarah stood beneath the canopy of the Great Tree with her friends, hands hovering over the twins. There was nothing she could do. They had to make their own decisions while the ritual was prepared around them.

The Shom still lingered in the air, a breeze that ruffled fur and hair alike but left her untouched. At her feet, Adrian's eyes still glowed with a silvery light over his damp muzzle. Lily stood, carrying Adrian in one hand while her other reached for Sarah's. Lines of a wind she could not feel appeared around them. Forms appeared. Wolves made of shadow ran after a trail of red mist. Behind them, three riders followed. Catherine led the group, the cowl of her cloak thrown back to show teeth bared in a snarl that could match any beast.

Ivy stamped the ground as her ears flattened against her head. "They're moving so fast..."

"That simply means that we will have to move faster," Alexandra said. From his belt he produced a small flask of glittering oil. Going before the tree he placed a hand on the roughened bark. His eyes shimmered with silvery light for a single moment before he turned his hand over and caught a golden acorn that dropped from the branches.

The acorn, once put in the oil, dissolved away leaving the liquid as clear as it had been before. With his hand, he applied the oil first to himself, then to each of them in turn. Three rays falling from a spiraling sun where drawn on each forehead with the oil. Sarah, the last to receive the touch, shuddered as the oil felt both cold and hot on her skin. The world wavered and blurred, the boundary between the material world and the Shom becoming thin. Alexandra and Lily steadied her.

"Can you do this? You connection to the Shom is nearly severed by your curse."

"You can tell?" So he had understood. That look in his eyes and the concern in Lily's hadn't been imagined.

"Anyone with the Sight could see it. Can you do this? Do you know what to do?"

She needed to think. Thinking had become hard as the chilling heat had become a dull pain. Behind the pain, a reassuring voice was whispering to her. It was encouraging her, telling her exactly what she needed to do. "Yes...I need your ritual dagger."

Alexandra handed it to her without another word. The leather wrapping of the hilt was soft with age, but not worn. The blade, bronze and etched with shallow troughs, shown as though freshly polished. The pain sharpened, her curse trying to reject the magic of the oil, so she tightened her grip on the hilt focusing on the feel of the leather and the whispers of knowledge the oil gave her. Alexandra stepped back, keeping an eye on her as he began to pour the herbal salts for the ritual to commence.

As one, the shoshyuh of the five houses looked to the tree, it's whispers guiding them to the words to empower the salt as it was poured. As conduit and boundary, it would protect them for a time from the outside interference, but only if the circle was complete—in blood and mind. Five circles were made in the salt, each linked with chains of ancient runes. It was a magic not seen since the time of the Five Sisters. A breeze that sighed through the heavy boughs overhead, and the ritual began:

"Here was were the first shoshyuh was created," Arya said, perched on a branch that had been stuck in the center of one circle.

"And here is were the last will be harvested," Alexandra followed.

"Here it began," Ivy whispered, her head low to the ground.

"And here we will be free." Sarah said for Lily.

"Blood for blood, so will it be." Adrian ended the incantation.

The conduit was complete. The salt mixture darkened as it was empowered, charring the grass beneath it. Sarah grit her teeth and kneeled, gripping the dagger even tighter. Adrian didn't look at her, his eyes had closed as he waited for the end. The whispers guided her, helped her lift the dagger over her friend's heart. The blade hesitated. No, she hesitated.

Adrian opened a silent eye to look at her. There was no malice, no anger at his situation. Sarah blinked the tears away, letting them roll down her cheeks. A question simmered just blow the surface, lodged in her throat behind a sob she wouldn't release. With a silent nod, he answered her, and the eye closed once more.

Down she thrust the blade. Adrian flinched and lurched beneath her. A yelp forced from the body at the violent blow. Once again their voices rose in unison, guided by the knowledge of the first shoshyuh. Behind their voices the howl of shadow wolves rose like a tidal wave to crash against the doors of the house. Servants screamed, and the wind roared around them, but inside of the circle the air was still.

Keep going, the voice whispered. *You will be safe.*

The first shadow beast entered the courtyard as Sarah removed the head. A bough of the tree, struck by the hound, cracked as she removed the first paw. They couldn't touched the circle. They couldn't break the conduit directly. They could, however, attack anything outside of the ritual space.

With branches reaching far over the roof of the house, the tree became the focus of the attacks. Hound after hound emerged from the shadows to claw and mar the Great Oak. When the hounds failed to do much, great snakes and bears appeared to strip and break the ancient wood.

The guiding whispers grew fainter.

Ivy squealed, prancing in place as she fought the urge to bolt.

"Stay strong," Sarah called as the inner doors flew open to the garden. "They can't touch you as long as you stay in the circle."

"But I can touch you," someone crooned from the doorway. "I can touch and eat every one of you."

Catherine emerged from the shadows, the pupils of her wide eyes pinpoints as she watched them. Drool and spittle dripped from her chin. Sarah shuddered, dropping the third paw beside the others. She knew that face, it was the same that had loomed over her father's body. The same that fed her the wolf's flesh.

Before Catherine could goad her, a bough of the tree came crashing down dangerously close to the lines of blackened salt. Alexandra flinched, one of the branches striking him as it broke apart. Catherine smiled in gruesome delight as the scratches on his face welled with blood.

Sarah cut away the final paw. She couldn't let Catherine distract her now. The voice of the tree was becoming fainter, as was Ivy's composure. The hounds pressed close to the boundary of the ritual space, parting only enough for Catherine to step forward.

But Catherine couldn't step forward. Vines wrapped around her feet, thorns sinking in to take hold of her clothes. A feral, enraged scream tore from the matron's throat. Ellen, her silvery hair stained with blood, stepped from the shadows as Sarah continued to work. The sharp ache in her skull deepened. The world dimmed for a moment, the pain mixed with the rolling nausea as she placed each part of her friend it it's proper place.

"All off the hounds, Catherine," Ellen warned called above the chanting of the shoshyuh.

"Ellen." The name came out as little more than a snarl. "I should have killed you the moment you refused to fell the tree."

"Nicolas did not need to die," she said. "And he does not need to die today—nor do any of these children."

Catherine's laugh pierced through the pain. A man lay in pieces before her, twisted into an animal shape by curses disguised as blessings. Her hands and clothes were stained with the blood of her friend, the only person to help her feel like more than a burden. Yet...Catherine was laughing. The Shom was gathering into Adrian's body now, dissolving the flesh and bone into a red and gold mist. The pain pulsed, so strong that she dropped the ritual knife to hold her head. Like a heart it beat and pulsed but with so much force it felt like her head would break open if she did not hold it.

Her part was done. The rest was on the others. And as the chanting rose, so did the mist swirling to envelope them in a small inferno. Catherine and Ellen's argument was lost in the burn of magic. Their shouting and screaming was nothing in the roar of the Shom. The pain, the pressure, it reached a crescendo within her. Something broke under the strain and the Shom that had been swirling around her surged forward, filling the void within her with a searing fire.

Sarah screamed. Her voice joining the others as they too were burned. Flakes of skin, hair, and flesh peeled away. The leaves and bark of the great tree broke free and swirled around them—a wall to obscured them from the world outside. Feathers, fur, hair, it was all burning away. Their ties to the bloodlines dissolved. The conditions placed on them broke down.

Then...the Shom rebuilt.

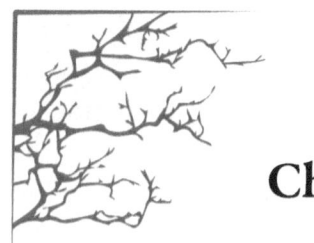

Chapter 16

T he world came back in fragments. Her feet were wet, grass prickled her soles and ankles. Blood that the ritual hadn't consumed had soaked into the ground. The ground tilted, and she fell to her knees, letting the blood creep up her simple gray gown. Adrian wasn't a fox anymore, and he was whole, but...

Lily's wail broke through the air. The wind responded in a spiraling maelstrom that tore away the lingering mist. Around her, still in their circles where the other shoshyuh, but only Ivy and Alexandra had remained the same. The bird and tree had each been replaced by a human, and Lily's golden locks had changed to a bronze.

Catherine's voice cut through the maelstrom, "What have you done?!"

The Shom hadn't fully disappeared. Remnants swirled around her matron like ribbons of iron. Cuts began to bleed from her cheeks, her arms, and her legs. Her robes and dress were being reduced to rags by the second. Where the great tree once stood, a young man stepped forth. His eyes glowed with a somber light as the wind continued to whip around them.

Ellen, tears shining on her cheeks, fell to her knees before the young man. "Nikolas."

A feint smile appeared. "Ellen, my darling..."

"Release me," Catherine hissed. "By the blood of the Five-"

"*My Sisters*," he said, his smile fading away, "The very same you call upon, are restless in their tombs. Someone brought their kingdom to ruin."

"The kingdom was already in ruin. The Rhogrik King had killed your father and mother, and the villages were in flames."

"And you pushed it over the edge for your own slice of power. Tell me," the prince's voice lowered, barely audible over the storm, "did you feel remorse for even a moment, when you took my sister's head to the barbarian king?"

Catherine glared at him. The gale winds that whipped around Sarah obscured her response. Whatever her response was, however, made the prince look away.

"May your greed consume you," he said and stepped away to help Ellen to her feet.

Catherine screamed curses as the remnants of Shom dug deeper and tore apart her form. Each lash bled crimson and gold, as if the souls of shoshyuh she had consumed were trying to escape. Her body contorted from pain, falling to the ground. The shadow hounds vanished, scooped up by the magical storm. Birds of prey, with feather glittering silver and gold, dove into the courtyard. Sarah looked away, unable to watch the judgment of the Feyse matron unfold.

Beside her, Lily keened as she pulled her brother's still form into her lap. Sarah pulled her close, Adrian's head lolling between them. "I'm sorry." It was all she could think. All she could say. "I'm so sorry."

As the wind died down, an uncanny silence filled the courtyard. Alexandra and Nicolas stood silently with Ellen. Arya, now a young woman with brassy auburn hair, stood beside Ivy, a large hawk on her shoulder. They were free. They could leave to run wild. Or they could stay. They had a choice now.

But as Sarah held Lily under the starlight, with the blood soaking through their simple gowns, she realized they were in no position to make that choice yet. They needed to hold a funeral, to set the past at rest. Only then could they look toward the future.

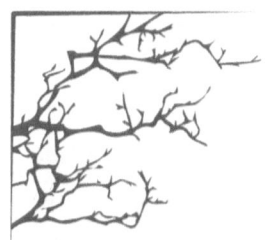

Epilogue

H e didn't know when he started to feel it, that shadow that crept along like a chill breeze. Below him, a presence stirred. Its hunger seeped through the ground. It called to him, sticky sweet with offerings of quiet oblivion. With a shudder, he floated away from the courtyard, into the mansion were servants were still recovering from the shock of the night.

That presence never wavered. It was like a void had taken form beneath the earth. It was everything the Shom could not be—empty, hungry, consuming in all ways. It called to him like a prayer for oblivion, like a prisoner's need for peace.

"Will you be staying?"

Adrian considered it, but didn't respond to Prince Nicolas. He was listening to Sarah and Lily, who cried behind the closed doors. His body was in there, carefully wrapped to appear whole again.

"Your sister," Nicolas continued, "were you close?"

That was an understatement. Adrian narrowed his eyes at the prince.

He raised his hands. "Easy. I'm already spoken for."

"What do you want?" His voice was little more than a whisper to his own ears, though he had tried to speak with a normal voice.

"To know your decision. It will be important for my own decisions."

"And what is it you are debating?"

"How to convince them to stay," Nicolas continued. "Adrian, I wasn't turned into a tree to protect the kingdom from the invading force. I was turned into a tree because there is something else, a force that consumes the Shom to survive. I was using my magic to keep it fed and sedated through my roots, but in this form...it's difficult. I need the other shoshyuh to stay and help me keep the beast contained."

Adrian paused, eyes wide as he considered the prince's words. So that was what he had felt in the courtyard, what whispered to him even now. "What happens if it can't be contained?"

"Then people will begin to die. Starting with those that have the weakest control of the Shom."

He bit his lip, or he would have if he had a physical body any more. As it was he was a ghost that hadn't realized what the repercussions of breaking all shoshyuh curses would be. What could he do but agree to stay and help his friends and family—even in death?

"I see you made your decision," Nicolas said. "Should I teach your sister to see the dead as I do?"

"Yes, but let her mourn first. I don't want her and Sarah trying to bring me back and sacrificing what little time we may have."

With a bow, Nicolas left. Adrian floated to the roof of the manor. It was lonely, the way the stars twinkled without the moon. But he new the moon was still there, could feel it though he could not see it. He supposed that's what he was to become now. An unseen guide in an unknown future.

Acknowledgement

Each story, like each year, comes with its own challenges. I nearly gave up on this story. The challenges of writing even part of a con-lang were larger than I first believed. It was only once I peeled back the excess and focused more on the core of the story, the journey of Adrien to save his family at the cost of himself, that I was able to put words to the page again.

Thank you, first and foremost, to my husband for his love and support during all of the ups and downs this journey.

Thank you to my nanas for their encouragement and patience in the writing process as well as My close friends, Darrell, Jason, and Din were also critical for their quiet support. A special thanks goes to my mother, who reads my newsletters even on our worst days.

And thank you, dear reader, for reading The Golden Fox.

About The Author

Valerie Lillis

A

storyteller from youth, Valerie Lillis has years of experience crafting worlds of fantasy and has become known for her believable dialogue and worldbuilding. She lives happily married with her husband and furbabies in Central USA. When not writing or spending time with her family, she enjoys listening to music while knitting scarves and small dolls.

Grimm Retellings

To Bloom in the Shadows

A queen's illness drives an arranged marriage between the kingdoms of Vedivin and Everautumn. Twenty-one years later, Renee and Sebastian meet to fulfill that contract and immediately Lust for one another. However, lust won't be enough to see them through the challenges, assassination attempts, and surprise pregnancy that await them. It's only after they find and embrace the Love between them that they are finally allowed to marry and solidify the union between their two kingdoms.

Requiem of a Queen

A queen must take on many responsibilities. Her culture, her entire history, could become meaningless to the growth of a kingdom. Treasured stories held throughout youth are challenged. Enemies become allies, and loved ones betray even the most intimate secrets. With an ailing father, Princess Annabelle is about to learn just how fragile her world is. With a mother who wants her head and a guardsman who wants her hand, it becomes a dance with death to keep her kingdom from falling into ruin.

The Golden Fox

Five families. Five dead princesses. A soul that refuses to pay and a soul that refuses to be sold. Adrian thought he understood the world he had been born into and the house he had been born to lead. But when his mother comes to him, the words "you've been chosen" on her lips, he realizes that he understood nothing.

He loses everything...except his life. And now he must fight to keep that, and the lives of so many others, too.

Praise for the Author

I really appreciate how much thought went into it world building wise...my only complaint is that I didn't want it to end!

- PRAISE FOR TO BLOOM IN THE SHADOWS

I couldn't put it down and can't wait to read the rest! Had me hooked from page 1 and excited to see where it goes.

- PRAISE FOR NEPHILYM

A well-written piece of short fiction that has an abundance of heart, emotion and lore not often seen nowadays. It keeps you turning the page and devouring more until there's nothing left, with a yearning to know more about the world but satisfied with the end nonetheless.

- PRAISE FOR THE RED KNIGHT

Connect with the Author

Consider joining my newsletter[1] to know when future stories of shadows and magic are released.

Website: valerielillis.com[2]

Mastodon: @Valerie_Lillis[3]

Instagram: VLillis.Writes[4]

---

1. https://dashboard.mailerlite.com/forms/713926/108929289271904099/share

2. https://www.valerielillis.com/

3.   https://indieauthors.social/@Valerie_Lillis

4.   https://www.instagram.com/VLILLIS.WRITES/